RESERVATION FOR MURDER

A Kyle Callahan Mystery

MARK McNEASE

Praise for *Last Room at the Cliff's Edge*

"Nathaniel Hawthorne wrote that 'easy reading is damn hard writing.' McNease writes in this ostensibly effortless way, employing all the elements of a true story teller: intrigue, tension, memorable characters and perfect pacing. I also admire the ease with which he captures a woman's point of view. Linda is heroic and flawed and utterly believable."

- Jean Ryan, author of *Survival Skills* and *Lost Sister*

"This suspenseful series launch from McNease (the Kyle Callahan Mysteries) introduces retired homicide detective Linda Sikorsky … Plausible sleuthing and smart characterizations combine for a winner."

- Publishers Weekly

Praise for *The Cat in the Window*

"… truly excellent – New Yorker-worthy, one might say. It was a perfect little Sunday-morning read."

- Michael Craft, author of *Inside Dumont* and *The Mister Puss Mysteries*

Also By Mark McNease

Audiobooks
Beautiful Corpse
A House in the Woods
Black Cat White Paws
Murder at Pride Lodge
Pride and Perilous
Death by Pride
Death in the Headlights
Last Room at the Cliff's Edge
Stop the Car

Mysteries and Thrillers
Beautiful Corpse
A House in the Woods
Black Cat White Paws
Murder at Pride Lodge
Pride and Perilous
Death in the Headlights
Death by Pride
Kill Switch
Last Room at the Cliff's Edge

Other Books and Writing
Stop the Car: A Kindle Single
The Seer: A Short Story
Rough & Tumble: A Dystopian Love Tragedy
An Unobstructed View: Short Fiction
5 of a Kind: More Short Fiction

MARK McNEASE

ACKNOWLEDGEMENTS

Thanks to my husband and forever beta reader, Frank Murray. As we approach our 14th anniversary, I can't think of anyone I would rather go through time with.

Thank you to my invaluable proofreader Bruce Halford, whose sharp eye has helped ensure there will be very few disruptions for the reader.

And thank you always to fans of the books, whose emails keep me going when I need it most and expect it least.

For Lee Lynch, friend and legend.

PART I

A New Beginning

PROLOGUE

Dear David:

Thank you so much for the birthday card. The big six-oh! I remember thinking at twenty-five how old forty would be, and now forty seems young and distant. Young because I wish I had the energy I had at that age, and distant because it is. The idea of twenty years shortened by fading memories into a slideshow of the past two decades is hard to express. And you and I had known each other so many years by then!

I hope you and Elliot are finding Los Angeles to your liking. How is his father's health? Moving there to take care of him was an amazing thing to do. I know from our conversations it was a difficult but necessary decision. My mother and her second husband Farley are in Scottsdale now, and I can't imagine moving there to take care of her if anything happened to him. We would if we had to, of course, but why ponder these things at all? It's like expecting heartache, or anticipating the things we dread most. For you and Elliot, I hope only that you like it there and that you're happy. The new grandchild helps, I'm sure, and having Elliot's son in Santa Barbara has to be a plus. I always knew you'd find the man of your dreams (for who is that but the one who brings us contentment?), and you did. We both did, and we're both at a time of life that's changing, new, exciting, and more than a little frightening.

We're leaving New York City at last. We've been driving back and forth to Lambertville for the past few months, getting the apartment ready to sell, and, to be honest, dragging our feet just a bit. New York has been my home since I moved here with you all those years ago, and for Danny even longer. But everyone's gone now. We seem to be the last two people on the train. His parents moved to Florida two years ago (shoot me if I ever suggest it). My beloved boss Imogene has packed up and flown the coop, teaching now in Santa Clarita. She has a sister there. Margaret Bowman passed away last Christmas. We went to both memorial services – one in Fort Lauderdale where she'd made so many friends, as Margaret was bound to do, and one here at the restaurant. You should have seen the crowd! The previous two mayors were there, along with celebrities, a few icons in the New York restaurant business,

4

you name it. She got the sendoff she deserved, and a week later we decided it was time to move, to face the sadness of leaving our home for a new one, but also to embrace the adventure.

We sold Margaret's Passion to Chloe Sparks. You remember her, she was the best assistant Danny ever had running the restaurant, and a fine woman. It's called Chloe's Gramercy Park now, and it's a success. What else would it be? We've kept the building for the income from the tenants, but the restaurant is all Chloe's and we're very proud of her.

At last the apartment has been sold and we have to vacate this week. Sad? Yes. Regrettable? Not at all. We've had our bed and breakfast, Passion House, in operation for two months. It's a huge learning curve with no end in sight, but I like that. I'm out of the TV business. My friends, including you, have all moved on. And I love Lambertville. New Jersey is such a beautiful state, and the Delaware River Valley is spectacular. I wish you'd seen it before you moved, but I also know you'll visit. Soon? Summer is your favorite season, and a great time to see such a beautiful town.

I'll let you go now. I so enjoy our letters. No one writes them anymore, everything's email and text. I do plenty of that, too, but old fashioned letter writing is something to savor.

I'll write you next from our home in Lambertville. We've got a big week coming up with a convention in town and Passion House is booked solid. I'm happy, Danny's happy, our new kitty Wilma is happy (God rest Smelly's little cat soul, we miss her still), and I don't imagine I'll be running into any serial killers in Lambertville! I've enjoyed the past few years without them, and if I never encounter another one it will be too soon. That was the old life, this is the new one.

Give my love to Elliot. Our best room is yours anytime, on the house. Or should I say on Passion House. I think Margaret would be happy we named it that, and I know Danny is.

Until we write again …

Love,

Kyle

CHAPTER 1

Kyle Callahan stood by the apartment doorway staring at what now seemed like vast emptiness. The movers had finished ten minutes ago and were already on their way out of the city.

"We have to go," he said to his husband Danny Durban. "We're meeting them at Passion House and we need to be there."

"You don't have to state the obvious," Danny replied.

Kyle knew the move was even harder on Danny than it was on him. The apartment had been Danny's long before he met Kyle thirteen years ago. Kyle and his cat, Smelly, had moved in from their home in Brooklyn. They'd been the new members of a family that had previously consisted only of Danny and his cat Leonard. It hadn't taken long, either. The men had been dating for three months when they decided to combine households, and that household had just been sold. They were vacating because they no longer owned it and the new residents were coming the next day. All the empty space Kyle was looking at, freshly painted, scrubbed, *cleansed* of their presence, had held memories until this very moment. Now those memories were ghosts who had to leave with them. The furniture and belongings they'd decided to keep would still provoke the same sentiments—the coffee cups Kyle bought from every place they'd traveled, Danny's awards for his years in the restaurant business—but they would not be housed in the same place. They, like their owners, were being uprooted by choice and planted in new ground.

"Are we doing the right thing?" asked Danny, standing next to Kyle with only the front door between them and their new life.

Danny was shorter than Kyle by six inches, and just a little over a year older. Kyle had fallen in like the first night they'd met at a dating event, and within weeks the like had turned to something close to love, or at least the anticipation of it. They were both thirteen years older now, and their added age, along with their height difference, was something Kyle never noticed except in photographs.

"There is no wrong thing, Danny. Everyone's gone. Some of them have left the planet. Time only goes in one direction and we're going with it. Let's be excited."

"I am excited. It's just hard. All those years in one place. This isn't just change. It's upheaval. I'm a city boy moving to the country. Who would ever have guessed that?"

Kyle put his arm around Danny. "Lambertville is not the country. Linda and Kirsten live in the country," he said, referring to their friends who had a small house in the woods outside Stockton, New Jersey. "We're moving to a fabulous, artistic, vibrant town we both love. And we already live there!"

The couple had been travelling back and forth the past three months between Lambertville, where they'd already opened their bed and breakfast, and Manhattan, where leaving had not been an overnight proposition: there had been the restaurant to deal with, the building they owned, and a thousand details that had to be dealt with when settled lives moved from one place to another.

"We should go," Kyle said gently.

He sensed Danny was crying silently. Just a tear or two.

"Joy and grief are not mutually exclusive," Kyle said. "Remember, when one door closes ..."

"Oh, for godsake, I hate that expression," Danny said.

"I know you do. That's why I said it."

The mood had lifted slightly and Kyle knew it was time. He turned and opened the door, taking in yet another view he would not see again: the hallway. They'd known their neighbors, and their neighbors' children and pets, all in this hallway, on the other floors and in the lobby. Life in a New York City apartment building was a microcosm of the city itself, teeming with personalities and lives grand and small.

A moment later they were outside the apartment. Kyle handed Danny the key.

"Here, you should be the one to do this."

Danny nodded. He took the key and locked the door.

A short elevator ride later they were at the front desk. Danny gave their key to Freddy, the morning shift doorman.

"You'll be back," Freddy said, trying to put the best face on a goodbye that was hard for the staff, too. Doormen, porters, handymen, the super—some of them spend their entire working lives in one building. They see new apartment owners settle in. They see the tenants' children grow up. They see the old ones die. And they see some of them leave.

"No, Freddy," said Kyle. "We won't. But I appreciate the thought. We're going to miss you, too. Tell your wife I want some of those cakes for the bed and breakfast."

"You serious, Mr. Callahan?"

"Of course we are!" Danny chimed in. "Nobody makes cakes like Loretta. We want them for our guests. How else can we make sure they come back? Now here—"

He pressed the key into Freddy's palm.

"—we'll call you in a few weeks to say hello. Tell Loretta to pre-heat the oven."

Freddy got up from behind the desk. He looked around nervously, as if he didn't want to violate any rules, then hurried to Kyle and Danny and hugged each of them.

"You'll be missed, really," he said.

"You will be, too," Kyle replied. "Remember, any time you and Loretta need a nice getaway, Passion House is yours."

"That's too kind, we'd love that."

Kyle knew Freddy would never take him up on it. It had been hard just getting people from Manhattan to come to Brooklyn when he lived there. The island was the center of the known universe for most people who lived on it. He knew doormen seldom resided in the city, but they were still city people. Lambertville might as well be Petticoat Junction to them. That's how he and Danny had thought of it until their first visit. Love at first sight had changed their minds.

A moment later they were in their car, a Toyota they'd purchased for their new life. You don't need a car in New York City, but life outside it is nearly impossible without one. Then came the drive cross town, a short delay into the Lincoln Tunnel, out the other side, and off into their new life.

CHAPTER 2

Passion House Bed & Breakfast was originally built as a single-family home in 1929 by one of Lambertville's wealthiest residents. Noah Habermeier had been a German immigrant who'd settled first in Newark, New Jersey, before finding the city too large and sinful and moving his family to the small river town. Noah was known for his religious piety and his capitalism, demonstrating an equal conviction for both. Prayer and profit were sacred to the father of ten, and in Lambertville he found the perfect place to start a general mercantile store that would later spread throughout the Northeastern states and presumably make the Habermeier heirs comfortable for life. Changing trends and technology saw the collapse of his retail empire, resulting in the eventual destitution of many of his grand- and great-grandchildren who, by the time Kyle and Danny bought the house, had been forced to work for a living and in most cases leave the area.

Located on the Delaware River in the southwestern part of Hunterdon County and now technically a city, Lambertville had undergone several transformations. During the 18th century local places were sometimes named after operators of ferries taking travelers across the river into Pennsylvania. Once known as Coryell's Ferry, after the ferry owner Emanuel Coryell, the community was renamed Lambertville in 1814 in honor of John Lambert, another famous resident, who'd served as United States Senator and Acting Governor of New Jersey. In more recent times Lambertville was not considered much of a place to be or visit, but during the 1990s the town began sprouting art galleries, antique shops, restaurants, and more than its share of charm.

Kyle and Danny first visited Lambertville when they were staying for a long weekend with their friends, Linda Sikorsky and Kirsten McClellan. Linda had been a police officer for the New Hope, Pennsylvania, Police Department, making her way up to Detective over the course of a twenty year career. She'd met the men seven years ago when she had investigated a murder at Pride Lodge, a popular LGBT resort in the area. They became fast friends, and when Linda retired, moving to a small house in the New Jersey countryside just twenty minutes from Lambertville, Kyle and Danny became regular houseguests. By then Linda had met and fallen in love with Kirsten, once a local real estate powerhouse and now an author writing mysteries in the woods while her wife ran a "vintage everything" store in New Hope. The two couples could often be seen eating in their favorite restaurants in both towns and walking across the bridge that connected them.

Approximately a year ago, Kyle and Danny began having conversations about getting older and what, if anything, they wanted to change in their lives. So many of the people they knew and loved had moved on or passed away. Manhattan had begun to feel like a ghost town of eight million living souls. Their restaurant, Margaret's Passion, had been Danny's other true love, but with its founder and namesake dead, his heart wasn't in it anymore.

"We need to do *something*," Kyle had said one night over dinner at home. "Go somewhere."

The thought of leaving New York had been preposterous just months before. Danny had lived there all his life, and Kyle had been there for almost forty years. But now, suddenly, it felt like the past. Kyle was staring at his sixtieth birthday coming at him full speed, and Danny had already gotten there. Why not make a move? Why not roll the dice at least one more time? They'd gambled on buying the restaurant and the building it was in. They'd taken a chance living together with the highest hopes but nothing guaranteed, at least in the beginning. That had worked out spectacularly well. All of it had worked out. So when they were walking around Lambertville on another visit to see Linda and Kirsten, a "For Sale" sign in a yard caught their attention. The house was huge – three stories with a large yard and a wraparound porch. It was also very run down. Someone kept the lawn and landscaping up, but that was to be expected in a town that considered it a civic responsibility. There was also a small guest house in back, which Kyle later learned had been built for servants at a time when it was common for rich people to have them.

Kyle had a vision in the moment, standing on the porch peering into the empty rooms: a bed and breakfast.

"You're out of your mind," Danny had said. "And let's get off the porch. Somebody might be home."

"Nobody's home," Linda said from behind them. All four of them were now staring through the large front window. "No one's lived here for years. I think the family still owns it, or maybe the bank. You'd have to call the real estate agent to find out, but I bet you can get it for a steal."

Danny saw her smile and knew a plot had been hatched then and there to convince him to embark on one of the biggest adventures — and risks — of his life.

That had been in August of the previous year. Over the course of the next eight months they transformed the nearly-dilapidated, one-time mansion into Passion House, a bed and breakfast that was fully operational by the time they left their apartment in the city for the last time. By springtime it was staffed, bringing in income and challenging them on a daily basis. Kyle loved it. And he saw that Danny loved it, too. It had given them new life and new direction. They lost their beloved cat, Smelly, to age and infirmity. Their other cat, Leonard, was still going strong and they'd gone so far as to adopt a new one named Wilma. Leonard didn't seem to mind the new feline in the family, which had been as important as their own reaction to her. And this week, two months after opening, they had their biggest booking yet. Three of the five rooms were already occupied, thanks to a reduced weeknight rate, and the two upstairs suites were booked for arrival the next day.

Counting the guests on his fingers, Danny had said, "Nine people in our house at the same time. That's really scary."

"That's really successful," Kyle had replied as he drove through Flemington. It was a trip they'd made dozens of times but would not be making again, except when they wanted to visit old friends or spend a day in the city. "We'll be fine. We've got Justin and Patty. And we live in the guest house. We don't have to spend time with any of them, except for breakfast and if they need anything."

The guest house had been a godsend. They'd first thought of living on the third floor, but then decided, after talking to other bed and breakfast owners, that making their home in another location would be a sanity-saver. Luckily they had an option, and they'd made the small guest house as comfortable as their apartment had been, minus all the clutter they'd cleared away when they moved.

"This is a turning point for us with Passion House," Kyle had said. "If we're booked up once, we'll be booked up again and again. Stop fretting, we can do this."

Danny had sighed. He knew Kyle was right. If they hadn't believed they could succeed, they never would have taken the chance. This would be the real beginning of their new life.

When they bought the house it was an abandoned mansion in disrepair. The dark green exterior paint had been peeling for many seasons; the front porch had two lights that hadn't had working bulbs in them for years; and the guest house looked more like an especially large shed whose windows were too grimy to see through. They purchased the property from the bank, which had foreclosed on it two years earlier from the last remaining Habermeier, a woman named Grace who lived in Texas and had stopped making payments on a loan against the house. That was how they got it for such a good price, allowing them to invest an additional thirty-five thousand dollars into renovating it. The house went from being what its neighbors had called an eyesore, to a beautiful, interesting, new bed and breakfast with the unusual name *Passion House*.

"It kind of sounds like a place where senators meet their mistresses, or people stay to indulge their sexual fantasies."

Danny had bristled at Kyle's comment. "It's named after Margaret's Passion, and it's *our* new passion. I can't be bothered with other people's interpretations, and neither should you."

He'd been right, and Kyle had quickly let go of his concerns over the name. Passion House it would be, and Passion House it was, when the final touches were added and the gorgeous, hand-painted wood sign was planted in the front yard.

The house had five guest rooms, three on the first floor and two on the second. The rooms on the second floor had been turned into suites by combining smaller rooms the original inhabitants had probably used for sewing or reading. The third floor was off-limits to guests and included two rooms for the live-in staff as well as space for storage and supplies.

The suites had themes: one was the Manhattan Suite, with a mural of the New York City skyline on one wall, a sleek gas fireplace, and furnishings of chrome and glass that reflected a modern feel. Kyle had thought it was incongruous given their new location, but he knew Danny had wanted something to remind him of the life they'd known, a way of preserving it as the memories faded over time, so he'd said nothing when the mural was painted. Walls could always be painted again.

A second suite, called Margaret's Room, had been designed with Margaret Bowman in mind. Danny remembered her apartment above the restaurant and he'd had the room furnished as if it belonged to everyone's favorite old aunt. It included a large, comfortable overstuffed chair, a faux fireplace, and an afghan Margaret had given to Danny when she moved to Florida. There was a mural of the Delaware River Valley on one wall and rustic furniture that made the guests feel as if they were staying in the woods somewhere not far from the river. The standard rooms downstairs were all comfortable and tastefully decorated to reflect the kind of life you find in a quaint river town.

Unlike most bed and breakfasts, each room had a small flat screen TV. Danny and Kyle had the habit of watching TV when they slept, allowing it to shut off with a timer at the 1:00 am hour. They never stayed where there was not a television, and Danny said the guests who didn't want one could simply leave it off.

There were two shared bathrooms on the first floor, complete with tub and shower, while each room upstairs included a private bath. They'd hired a local jack-of-all-trades named Chip McGill to do some of the heavier renovations on the house, along with two men he paid to help him. One of them, a gay man in his late twenties named Justin Stritch, had subsequently taken the job of live-in handyman, moving into one of the third floor rooms. Justin had been a drifter by his own admission, having lived in several states since being rejected by his religious parents and banished as a teenager to life in the streets of Philadelphia. He'd survived well enough, moving around the country and finally settling in Lambertville, where he'd lived with two roommates for the past year doing odd jobs and handyman work. Kyle and Danny knew he might not stick around, given his history, but he was smart, reliable, hardworking and eager to be part of this new adventure.

The other live-in staff was a woman named Patty Langley. Originally from Lambertville, Patty have lived in Frenchtown, then Stockton, and even the big city of Princeton, finally coming back to her home turf a year ago. In her years serving other people, she'd been a nanny, a maid, a personal assistant, and an aide to a succession of elderly clients. They'd found her through a referral from one of their many new friends in town, and, as promised, she had proved to be exceptionally conscientious, if not very friendly.

By early April they were ready to open for business, and Passion House was birthed. The first week they had three guests in two of the rooms. The second week four. By their one-month anniversary in May they were getting enough bookings to think they might just pull this off, and now, as they returned from their last trip to Manhattan as residents, they were full to capacity and nervous. Everything needed to go right—no plumbing crises, no leaking roof, no conflict between guests. They'd discovered that most people staying in a bed and breakfast got along fine, but once in a while there were personality clashes, usually solved by the guests in question avoiding each other. They hoped for none of that this week as they pulled into the driveway, got out of their car and headed for the only home they had now.

CHAPTER 3

Scott Harris was excited about the trip. He hadn't been back to Lambertville in five years and had not expected to return. He didn't dislike the town, he'd just had enough of it growing up there, then staying as his twenties passed, his thirties, and finally his forties. He'd always had what he thought of as bigger dreams, although he'd never been able to define those dreams beyond getting rich, famous, or some combination of both. When he found himself working at a grocery store, a middle-aged man slicing meat and cheese for impatient octogenarians, he decided his life was over and dreams were for the foolish. Then, one day, a handsome older man (which at Scott's age meant in his sixties), number 42 from the ticket machine they used to serve customers, asked for a half-pound of Vermont Yellow Cheddar. Scott looked up at the person who'd placed the order. His eyes met those of Harold Summit, and love arced over the deli counter, striking them each in the heart. That Harold was rich and sort-of-famous, the author of a series of thrillers set in Los Angeles, made Scott rethink the death of his dreams. Maybe they'd just been on life support and Harold was the experimental treatment they'd needed. Harold, never a bashful man, wrote his cell phone number down on a business card and exchanged it for his bag of cheese.

Scott's manager Daphne was on duty that day. Fearful of being scolded for flirting with a customer, Scott discreetly tucked the business card into his apron and nodded politely at Harold, telling him to have a nice day. A last smile was exchanged as Harold wheeled his grocery cart around and walked slowly toward the dairy department.

Later that evening Scott could not believe his good luck. The business card read: Harold Summit, Author, Lecturer, Man of Letters. Then, as if one subtitle were not enough, it added in italics, *The Connor Dark Novels*. Not "mysteries," not "thrillers," but "*novels*." Hoping Summit was not as pretentious as his calling card, Scott dialed the number. What followed was a two-hour-long conversation with Harold that left them aching for more.

Harold was visiting Lambertville for old time's sake. He'd lived
there for many years before moving to Manhattan a decade ago to
pursue his career as a writer, with a second move to Los Angeles
more recently.

"I could have written from anywhere," Harold said, "but I
wanted to be in the thick of it, you see. I needed to feel the city, to
smell it. The bustle of Times Square, the stench of Hell's Kitchen.
My character Connor lives there, and it seemed I really should,
too. It's best to write about places you know intimately, you
understand?"

Scott nodded as if Harold could see him through the phone.
He noticed Harold had mentioned his fictional antihero as if he
were a living person but he gave it little thought, assuming
writers and artists were just odd that way.

"The series was a smashing success, as you know ..."

Actually, Scott didn't know — he'd never read a Connor Dark
novel but planned to remedy that immediately.

"I came back to visit friends in the city and we decided to
spend a few days at Pride Lodge. I went to the grocery store for
some provisions, I'm not one to eat every meal out."

Scott knew where Pride Lodge was, just a few miles outside
New Hope. He had availed himself of their large, popular
swimming pool in the summer, but never stayed there.

"Back to the city?" asked Scott. "I thought you lived there."

"I'm in Los Angeles now," came the reply. "For the past two
years, developing movie ideas and plans for a Connor Dark TV
series. It's in pre-production."

Scott's heart sank. This wonderful man, this cultured,
talented, *wealthy* man, was from the other side of the continent. So
why had he bothered flirting with Scott? Was he looking for a
one-night fling while he strolled memory lane in his old home
town, something to tell his friends about around a game of
Monopoly?

"I've never been to Los Angeles," Scott said, hoping he didn't
sound as disappointed as he felt.

"Then you must come."

"I must?"

"I insist."

"But I work in a deli. It would take me months to save up the
money for a trip." Taking a risk, he added, "Will you wait for me?

I could probably swing it by October."

"There's no reason to wait, Scott. Money is not an obstacle."

They were words Scott had never heard before.

"But I've always paid my way. I'm a proud man."

"And you can stay that way. I need an assistant, and I have no interest in the pretty young things one so often finds at the side of old men."

"Old*er*," Scott said.

He heard Harold laugh over the phone. "I'm not the pompous ass you might think from the business card. It's meant to be playful, even if I'm the only one playing. It also creates an appearance, when appearances and bullshit are half the game.

"I don't say 'older' when I'll be sixty-seven in a month. I'm not frightened by my own mortality like so many people you meet. I'm old, Scott, and unashamed of it. Now let's cut to the chase, as they say. I'd like to have dinner with you — we can go Dutch if it's important to you — and then I'd like to talk about your first trip to L.A. I'll need to interview you in my own environment, so to speak."

"Interview me?" Scott asked. "Is that what you want to do?"

He felt himself smiling.

"I'm sure you'll get a call-back," Harold replied. "So what do you say?"

What Scott wanted to say was, "When's the next flight?" Instead he said, "I'll think about it, Mr. Summit."

"'Mr. Summit.' I like that. But only in public if you take the job. In private you can call me Harold."

"I might call you Forty-Two," Scott replied.

"Forty-Two?"

"That was your number at the deli."

"Call me whatever you'd like to, just say yes."

"I have to think about it," Scott said, not needing to think about it at all. "I'll let you know over dinner. When, where, and what time?"

The following night they had an incredible meal at Marsha Brown in New Hope, which Scott allowed Harold to pay for. Complete with an excellent red wine and a bill for over $200, it provided evidence for Scott that money was indeed not an obstacle.

Five years, three novels and a canceled television series later they were back in Lambertville. Scott had moved to L.A. two months after meeting Harold. He'd accepted the job as the personal assistant to Mr. Summit and, two years later, as his husband. He'd also learned that Harold wasn't so unconcerned about being old that he didn't team with a younger writer named Bradley Manning to accompany him to industry meetings. He might not have a problem with his age but the money men and women of Hollywood weren't so accepting.

They were in town for a conference of the Mystery Authors Alliance being held at the Lambertville Station Restaurant and Inn. Harold maintained memberships in a half-dozen professional organizations, and MAA was one of them. The conference moved around from year to year, attempting to please a membership that included writers from all fifty states. It was pure coincidence they'd chosen a river town in New Jersey that had once been home to both Harold and Scott. Harold loathed staying in the hotels and convention centers where the meetings were always held, so they'd booked one of the suites at a new bed and breakfast in town.

"Passion House," Scott had said, when he was looking for a place to stay. "That's an intriguing name. And it's run by a gay couple."

Harold was accustomed to letting Scott make all the arrangements. That's what a personal assistant does.

"I like the name. Who doesn't need a little passion?"

Scott called that day and booked the room, making them the final guests in a full house. He'd spoken to Kyle Callahan, one of the owners, when he'd made the reservation. He could have done it online but preferred talking to human beings.

That was three weeks ago. Now, after a flight to Newark, a car rental and an hour's drive, they were parked in front of Passion House, early but pleased. The house looked marvelous. Scott gazed up at the second floor, where he'd been told their suite was, and wondered which window would be theirs.

"We're here," he said, reaching over and gently shaking Harold in the passenger seat.

Harold opened his eyes, adjusting back to consciousness. It had been a long day and he was ready for a power nap followed by a stroll through town.

"Do you think they'll let us check in early?" Harold asked,

unbuckling his seat belt.

"They always do," Scott replied. "Once they realize who you are."

"And if they don't know, I'm sure you'll tell them."

"It's my job, Forty-Two."

Harold did not like being called Forty-Two but he'd humored Scott for the past five years. He truly loved the younger man, having come to think of him as incredibly efficient and committed, offering a devotion Harold had not always returned. There had been dalliances, as there probably would be until Harold was no longer capable of performing or interested in other men. Scott had turned a half-blind eye, and in exchange Harold had provided him with an extremely good life.

They exited the car, Scott circling around to the trunk for the suitcases and laptop. He took a deep breath, convinced the air smelled of Lambertville, memories, and triumph. He'd come a long way on the road back home, and he'd come in style.

CHAPTER 4

"Gladys Finch is a legend in lesbian fiction," Kyle said. "And she's staying at our bed and breakfast!"

Danny was sitting across from him at the small table that was proportional to the size of their kitchen. Everything in the guest house was small. It had not been intended for comfort, since the butler and maid were there to work, not to enjoy themselves, and it had been up to subsequent residents of the main house to upgrade it. Danny and Kyle had done quite a bit of that themselves, with the help of Chip and Justin, and it could now be described as a cozy cottage for four: Kyle, Danny, and the two cats.

"I didn't know you read lesbian fiction," Danny replied dryly. He'd been going over the breakfast menu for the next few days, as well as plans for a book signing Thursday night. Kirsten McClellan's third Rox Harmony mystery had just been published and they were holding a reading at Passion House.

Kyle didn't appreciate Danny's tone. "I read *good* fiction. Gladys Finch is a master of the short story and a respected novelist. It could be beneficial for our brand if she likes it here."

Admitting Kyle had a point, Danny said, "Make sure to include something extra in her welcome basket."

All the guests were treated to a basket of jams, jellies and crackers from Dahl House Jams, a local operation run by a woman named Maggie Dahl who'd been among the first to welcome Kyle and Danny to Lambertville's business community.

"There's a whole shelf at Booketeria devoted to her books," Kyle said, referring to the town's popular bookstore. "We need to get some this morning and put them on the bookcase in the parlor. I'll bend the spines so they look read."

"What room is she in?"

"*They,*" Kyle said. "She's coming with her wife, Carol something ..."

"That's her name? Carol something?"

"I don't know her last name. I just know Gladys dedicated her most recent story collection to her. They're booked into the

Manhattan Suite, across the hall from the *other* big name writer, Harold Summit. We've already got a couple of his books in the parlor."

Kyle leaned forward and scanned Danny's menu upside down. "Can we pull this off?"

"A full house? Of course, we have to. This is what we do for a living now, Kyle. It's not a hobby."

Kyle sat back in his chair and sighed. They'd managed to stay in business for two months and had every intention of succeeding, but the stress of it was sometimes hard for him. They had five people already checked in, with four more on the way. They had plans for a book reading that would bring in another sizable group from outside, and four fabulous breakfasts to make before everyone checked out and headed home. The writers conference had been a gift for them, but it had also presented them with a first big test: keeping a house full of guests happy from the time they arrived until the time they drove off with Passion House in their rearview mirrors.

"Excuse me," Kyle said, getting up from the table. "I think I'm going to be sick."

"Don't be so dramatic," Danny replied, not looking up from his menu. "And please feed the kids."

Kyle said nothing else, heading to the cabinet for a can of cat food. The sound of the cabinet door opening was enough to bring Wilma running into the kitchen, her claws clicking on the tile as she slipped and slid in a mad dash for her food bowl. Leonard sauntered in a moment later, tail up, taking his time. He was old now and had no use for such foolishness.

Kyle had discovered quickly that running a bed and breakfast meant sometimes feast, and sometimes famine. There had been a few weeks when they only had one or two rooms booked, usually on the weekends, but they had to maintain the same cozy environment, with the same welcoming attitude, as if every night were booked solid and a breakfast table for ten with only four people at it was not the least bit awkward. If they only had a guest or two, or were out of town themselves for some reason, Justin and Patty would fill in, acting as their surrogates.

Patty Langley was a good cook, perfectly capable of taking

Danny's place when she needed to. She was also an outstanding housecleaner, room attendant, errand runner, and task master. Kyle learned quickly that keeping a house clean was much more difficult than keeping an apartment clean. For one thing, you could see everything in a house full of windows. Their co-op in Manhattan had faced the back of Baruch College, depriving them of a view but also of sunlight. Once they were living at Passion House, they couldn't escape the sight of dust and the everyday debris of living outside the city. Leaves fell, grass clippings flew. The next thing you knew, there were twigs inside your front door and you could coat your finger in dust just running it across an end table.

Patty was somewhere in her fifties, though she wouldn't say how far and would not take kindly to being asked. She was tall and thin; she wore her hair most days in a graying braid down her back, and she tended to dress in calf-length skirts, simple blouses and, when the weather was chill, a draping, button-down sweater she said her mother had given her many years ago. That the sweater was in good condition after such a long time was evidence of Patty's fastidiousness. She was hard to get to know because she kept her personal life and her professional life completely separate. That extended to living on the third floor of Passion House. She'd insisted on a lock on her door, which Kyle and Danny promptly installed, and she spoke only of her late mother, as if there had been no one else in her life for the fifty-plus years she'd lived it.

This all suited Kyle and Danny fine. They knew from the first day that running a bed and breakfast was hard work, requiring daily commitment. They needed people like Patty and Justin if they were going to succeed. Patty's work ethic was awe-inspiring, with Monday always strictly off. Sometimes she stayed in her room, with forays into town, and sometimes she simply vanished, returning Monday night to rest for the resumption of work the next morning. They had encouraged her to take a second day off, but the thought of not working for two days seemed unsettling to her, as if looking after Passion House gave her a reason for living.

Justin Stritch was another matter, and a polar opposite to the woman who quietly and quickly exercised authority over him. Twenty-six going on eighteen, Justin was the first person to tell you he was a free spirit and the last to admit that it meant immature. But he was a demon with a hammer and a wrench and could be called on any time of the day or night to appear with a toilet plunger. He was the fix-it guy, and a house as large and demanding as Passion House needed someone on-site. It saved Kyle and Danny from those 5:00 a.m. calls from guests who'd used a half roll of toilet paper or whose HDMI cable had come unplugged from their TV set.

One of the rules they'd laid down for Justin: no men in his room. Passion House had not been named for that kind of passion, and Justin was very much in his sexual prime. They knew from the grapevine that he had a fondness for no-strings sex. They refused to judge him for it, insisting only that he take his pleasure elsewhere, and never with a guest.

They were all a kind of family, with daddies Kyle and Danny living in the guest house with the cats. It was something neither man had expected, but both had come to enjoy, a sort of communal enterprise that enriched their lives in ways they'd never expected.

Everything was running smoothly and today all hands were required on deck. Danny had gone to the Giant grocery store in New Hope for supplies, with a stop at Booketeria to pick up a few of Gladys Finch's books. Patty was doing her daily inspection of the house. Justin was edging the lawn along the walkway. Kyle heard the edger stop and Justin say, "Good morning! Welcome to Passion House," a greeting he'd taken it upon himself to offer each and every guest.

Kyle looked at the clock on the parlor wall above a guest registry that sat on an oak pedestal. It was 10:00 a.m.

"Don't worry, the rooms are ready," a voice said.

Kyle turned, surprised to see Patty standing in the doorway with a dust rag. She was quiet in more ways than one, and had often startled them by being in a room without them knowing it.

"Thank you, Patty. You're amazing."

She cracked the slightest of smiles, then turned and walked down the hallway.

The front door opened, and in walked Scott Harris and Harold Summit. Kyle recognized Summit from his author's photo on the back of his books. The picture had been taken some years earlier, or possibly Photoshopped: the man was obviously a decade older than his headshot.

"I hope we're not too early," the younger man said.

"Of course we're not," Summit stated, as if someone of his stature could arrive whenever he pleased.

Kyle immediately disliked the man, but it didn't matter. "Not at all," he said. "Your room's been prepared."

"Suite," Summit said, frowning.

"Suite, yes." Stepping forward, Kyle extended his hand. "I'm Kyle Callahan, and this is Passion House."

CHAPTER 5

Gladys Finch had heard herself described as a literary icon so many times it didn't mean anything. She was one, of course. She'd been a pioneer in lesbian fiction when most people who were aware it existed thought Radclyffe Hall's *The Well of Loneliness*, with its antiquated classification of gay people as "inverts" and its plea to "Give us also the right to exist," was the gold standard. *Tarnished fucking gold*, she'd thought when she wrote her first lesbian short story sixty years ago. She was twelve years old at the time and knew exactly who she was and what she desired. Heterosexuality and conformity were not included.

A hundred short stories, two plays, and twelve novels later, she was tired of it all. Weary of travelling, of signing books, and especially of being considered some kind of living archive by young writers, many of whom had jettisoned the words "lesbian" and "gay" as labels for old people—like Gladys. She still called herself a dyke and refused to be cowed by today's genderqueers and non-binaries. She didn't have any problem with what they chose to call themselves, or, in modern parlance, *self-identify as*, but she'd be damned if she was going to identify herself as anything but a no-bullshit dyke, lesbian, and trailblazer.

She'd even resisted marriage for most of the thirty-five years she'd been with Carol Dupree, her longtime editor and now spouse. They'd married a month after the Supreme Court made marriage equality national, and Gladys was still not sure it had been the best decision. Gladys was seventy-two and Carol a mere sixty-three. She'd known Carol had coveted a marriage license for some time, but it wasn't until Carol had convinced her that a hostile nurse or some other stranger, at whose mercy they may find themselves, would be legally bound to treat them as spouses that she'd finally acquiesced.

Acquiesced. She liked that word. For Gladys was, if nothing else, a lifelong lover of words. She wasn't afraid to use them, either. It was not her problem if readers had to stop mid-sentence to look up a word she'd used. That was how she'd learned so many of them, reading difficult writers who did not write down to her. As a child, she'd spent more time with a dictionary than with a doll or some ridiculous toy oven, looking up words she'd read in books marred by underlining on every other page.

She hadn't intended to join the Mystery Authors Alliance. Given her stature, it had not required writing a mystery, which she told people was in the works. She'd even come up with characters and a plot, and when anyone asked, "Gladys, how's the mystery going?" she could throw out a scene description she'd invented in the moment, or say she was researching murder weapons. In truth, she had no intention of writing a mystery and had only tried her hand at it once, in a short story that never saw the light of day.

In a word, dreadful. That's what the editor of a small mystery magazine had told her. She hadn't tried for the big names, *Ellery Queen Mystery Magazine*, or *Alfred Hitchcock Mystery Magazine*, none of the well-known ones. She'd never taken rejection well, especially since it rarely happened to her, and that one had been short and brutal.

I suggest you stick to what you do well, Ms. Finch. In service of your talent, I have to say 'D' for effort.

That was twenty years ago. The story was promptly shredded and Gladys never again tried her hand at a mystery.

She'd joined the Alliance, and accepted an invitation to be on a panel discussing character development, specifically because of its membership list. Gladys had not come all the way from the warmth of Arizona, where her aging bones enjoyed year-round comfort, just to talk about making people up from thin air. She had come to confront. She wasn't so old she couldn't give as good as she got in a fight, and a fight is what she expected.

Gladys and Carol had flown into Philadelphia. It was closer to Lambertville than New York was, requiring a shorter drive. Gladys didn't ride well in cars anymore. Her hips, her legs, her ass, were not up to spending more than an hour or so in a passenger seat.

Carol, as chipper as ever, announced the road signs as they passed them, as if each exit led to a potential adventure. It was one of the things Gladys loved about her. An excellent editor and a fiercely devoted partner, Carol was nevertheless a little clueless.

Gullible, Gladys thought, another word she liked.

Driving north on 295, Carol read out the town names as they passed the exit signs, a hint of wonder in her voice. *Palmyra, Riverton, Holmesburg, Andalusia.*

"How about lunch in Andalusia?" Carol said. "That sounds fascinating, like 'the fields of Andalusia.' Imagine eating there."

"Among the war dead?" Gladys replied dryly.

"Excuse me?"

"It sounds like a battlefield. The fields of Andalusia. Or a Van Morrison song. I'll pass."

Carol frowned. "But aren't you hungry?"

"I'm more in need of getting out of this car than I am of eating. Let's just get there. We can eat in town. I'm assuming Lambertville has a restaurant or two."

"It's fabulous, from what I've read," Carol said. "Very artistic."

Gladys cringed. Artistic was not a selling point for her. It usually meant pretentious, ethnically homogenous and reeking of privilege. She couldn't name a single town she'd ever wanted to visit because it was "artistic."

Staring at the highway ahead of them, Gladys said, "How did you find this bed and breakfast we're staying at?"

"Facebook," Carol replied, as if it were obvious. "I posted about the trip and asked for suggestions, and someone said there's a new B & B run by a gay couple."

"So everyone there is gay?" Gladys asked, suddenly feeling better.

"I have no idea! I just know the two men who run it are. Kyle and Danny. They look good together—there's a photo on the About page—and they're sort of our age."

"You mean your age."

"You know I never think about our age difference. Age is just a number!"

Gladys cringed again. She hated empty platitudes, especially about aging. Getting old was awful, and the older she got, the more awful it was. She would not pretend otherwise.

They finally saw the sign for NJ-29, which ran along the Delaware River into Lambertville. Exiting, Carol said, "Not long now. We'll be there in twenty minutes."

Gladys took a deep breath. Every trip they took was a long

one, and this one had required extra patience. The flight, the drive, the almost unbearably upbeat mood of her wife, had all combined to exhaust her. Gladys wanted only to check in, take a nap, and plan her next move.

CHAPTER 6

By three o'clock that afternoon, Passion House was full. Both second-story suites were occupied, one with Scott Harris and Harold Summit, the other with Gladys Finch and Carol Dupree. Upon welcoming them to the house, Kyle immediately identified the dynamics in their relationships: Scott was both Harold's assistant and his husband, though it wasn't clear which role he played most. Gladys, likewise, was the star in her marriage, but unlike Summit, who'd eyed the large front parlor with displeasure, Gladys seemed uninterested in her surroundings, while Carol gushed about the furniture and what she quickly labeled the hominess of the place.

The remaining rooms were occupied by the types of guests Kyle and Danny normally got—another gay male couple downstairs, a young, opposite-sex couple, and a single, elderly gentleman who was in town tracing his genealogy and who kept entirely to himself.

"I love hanging the 'No Vacancy' sign out," Kyle said to Danny as they sat at their kitchen table that afternoon, "but nine people is a *lot* to deal with."

"We don't have to deal with them," replied Danny. "Just check them in and forget about them until breakfast."

"A toilet's going to clog, I just know it. Or someone's going to lose a key."

Each guest was given a key to the house, to be returned on checkout. Patty had instructions to lock the door at 10:00 p.m. for security purposes.

"That's what Justin and Patty are there for," Danny said.

The whole reason for having two onsite staff people was so Kyle and Danny could be as relaxed as possible about operating a business like Passion House. *Clogged drain? Justin can handle it. Need clean towels? Patty will get them for you right away.*

"I understand that," Kyle said. "I also know with that many people something is going to go wrong. Don't kid yourself, we'll be called into action before they're all gone."

"Of course we will. We have breakfast to serve and Kirsten's reading tomorrow night."

Kyle had almost forgotten about the book reading. Kirsten's mystery series had sold well enough for her to have written three of them. Linda had confided in Kyle that she wasn't happy having a fictional character based on her previous life as a detective, but Kirsten was her wife, and writing had given her something to focus on, a passion of her own. Kirsten had taken on the responsibilities of arranging the reading and inviting people to come, and she'd told Kyle she was expecting twenty people from the area. If a few of the houseguests chose to attend as well, the parlor room would be full, with half the audience spilling into the dining room. He'd regretted suggesting it, but flyers had been passed out, a Facebook event had been posted, and there was no backing out.

"Just relax," Danny said, slipping a small piece of bologna to each cat. He enjoyed an occasional snack of the meat rolled up with a slice of cheese inside, and Wilma and Leonard had been waiting noisily at his feet for their share.

"That's easier said than done."

"Would you rather be back in the city?"

It was a question Danny had asked several times since they'd moved, a way of reminding Kyle they both wanted this life change.

"No," Kyle said. "I'm happy here."

"So be happy."

Wilma reached up on her hind legs, pawing at Danny's leg for another piece of meat. He pinched off a small bit and handed it to her.

Justin had been warned, as nicely as a warning can be given, not to fraternize with the guests. His reputation had preceded him, almost costing him the job.

"He's cute," Danny had said after their first formal interview with the young man. "Is that going to be a distraction?"

"For who?" Kyle had asked, smiling.

"Not me!" Danny had replied, feeling called out by his husband. "My eye does not wander."

"Of course it does. Everyone's does, and it's okay. But I say we give him a chance. I called his references, I spoke to Chip about him, and he's obviously good at handy work."

"I bet he is."

"Oh, stop," said Kyle. "We just have to make it clear he is not here for any extracurricular activity. Not in the house, and not with the guests."

They'd been as direct about it as they could be, and so far Justin had not broken the rules.

Justin wasn't thrilled with the size of his room, but it was better than having roommates. The job also provided free meals and a decent weekly salary. There was a small TV he seldom watched on top of a bureau. Everything Justin wanted to see, he could stream on his phone or the cheap laptop one of his appreciative gentleman friends had given him. Much of what Justin owned — clothes, the laptop, the phone — had been provided by men twice his age who enjoyed his company. He was chatty and flattering, and not insincere. *Flighty*, some called him. But he was not calculating. He did not take advantage of the kindnesses of these men, instead allowing them to give him gifts when they wanted to. He asked for nothing and had been given a lot. It was fun for him. It was also smart: by not making demands, he did not put himself in the position of owing anything. It was all for pleasure, never serious. If things got heavy, which they had only once, he broke it off. In that case he had convinced Lawrence, a very nice but needy man in his fifties, that theirs would be a doomed love made tragic by their age difference. He had managed to convince Lawrence that ending the affair was Lawrence's idea, and now when he saw him in town there were no hard feelings, just a fleeting sadness in the eyes followed by, "Take care, Justin, see you around."

Justin saw a lot of men around. In a town as small as Lambertville it wasn't hard to know most of the men who made up the gay community, at least by sight. Justin's was a familiar face, and to quite a few, a familiar body as well. His libido had not diminished since he'd first had sex at fourteen with another boy in school, a jock who ditched his girlfriend to make out with Justin every chance he got, then acted as if they'd never met when they crossed paths in the hallways. Justin hadn't cared. It was the beginning of his love of casual sex, a love that persisted to this day. He knew he could pursue it as long as it was outside Passion House. He had also not met any guest so far who would tempt him to risk his job. That was, until today.

He slipped his hand into the waistband of his shorts. Something was stirring. He spent most of his time in his room dressed in sweatpants or pajama bottoms, with his jeans on a hook on the the door in case someone needed him quickly.

It was the way he looked at me, Justin thought. *Like I didn't have any choice in the matter, like a command or something.*

But he's sooooo old.

Justin had no idea what age Harold Summit was, only that he was the oldest man he had ever been attracted to, and that was saying something. Never an ageist, Justin truly enjoyed the company of older men, including their bodies. But Summit was clearly a senior citizen, and under normal circumstances would not get a second look from Justin. Oddly, surprisingly, it had not required a second look. Harold Summit, upon being introduced to Justin and Patty and told they were the in-house staff, had stared at Justin with a sense of ownership Justin had never experienced before. It had been a look that said, "Resistance is futile." It had also not gone unnoticed by Harold's husband, Scott, who had quickly moved them on.

"Nice to meet you both," Scott had said, staring at Justin as if it had not been nice at all. "Let's get to the room, Harold. We need to unpack, and you've got a conference to prepare for."

Harold had smiled at Justin, making it clear they would meet again, most assuredly alone.

Damnit, Justin, he told himself, taking his hand back out from his shorts. *Don't do this.*

But he knew he would.

CHAPTER 7

"I thought you said they moved from New York."

Gladys was only slightly less grumpy now that they'd settled into their room. She'd left the unpacking to Carol, as she always did. She was sitting in one of two armchairs the suites provided, wishing it was more able to accommodate her bulk.

"That's what their About page says," Carol replied. She was as cheerful as Gladys was dour. She liked to think of it as the yin and yang of their relationship.

"So why have a mural of Manhattan on the wall? And what's with this furniture? It looks like it came from some twenty-year-old's apartment who couldn't afford anything but chrome and glass."

"It's called the Manhattan Suite," Carol said. "I'm sure they wanted it to have a city feel. We're not that far from it."

Gladys grunted. She'd been to New York many times and never liked it. She hated the summer smells of the place, the congestion, the people dashing madly from one very important meeting to the next, and the walking. New York was a walking city, and Gladys did not walk.

"Well, I wish you'd picked one of the other rooms."

"There are only two suites here, Dear, and I know you insist on staying in one."

It was true. Gladys had an expansive personality to match an expansive talent—just ask Gladys herself. She found most hotel rooms claustrophobic and always insisted on a suite. It was one of the few things she splurged on.

"Who's in the other one?" Gladys asked. "Maybe we can swap."

"I don't know who's in the other one, and I wish you would just accept it. We're here. We're going to have a good time. And you'll finally get to let the world know what happened to you!"

"You make it sound like pleasure."

"It is, admit it."

Carol was right and they both knew it. Gladys detested conventions in general, using them only as a marketing and promotional tool. She enjoyed being a celebrity fish in a not-too-large pond. And she would expose Harold Summit once and for all. Would it end his career? She doubted it. Would it disgrace him as the fraud and thief he was? She certainly hoped so.

For the first time in several days she smiled.

"It reminds me of my grandmother's bedroom," Scott said. They were settling into the Margaret Suite, the one Gladys Finch would have much preferred. Harold was standing by the window, looking out on the street below. "Minus the fireplace and the overstuffed chairs."

"And the coffee table, I presume," said Harold.

"Right, right, no coffee table in Nonny's bedroom."

"Of course you called her 'Nonny,'" Harold muttered.

"What, Sweetness?"

"Nothing."

Harold's mood had brightened only briefly since they'd arrived, during his quick encounter with the houseboy. He assumed that's what Justin was: a minimally useful handyman who doubled as eye candy for the couple who owned this place.

"Do you suppose they have three-ways?" Harold asked.

"Who are you talking about?"

Scott had their large suitcase on the bed and was unpacking it, putting Harold's carefully folded T-shirts, underwear and socks into the top drawers of the dresser.

"Kyle and Danny. That's their names, right?"

"It is," said Scott, "and I don't think it's any of our business." Hesitating a moment, he added, "I don't like that young man, Justin. He seems unsavory."

"You don't like any young men," Harold replied. He'd left his place at the window and taken a seat in one of the chairs. "You're the jealous type, Scott. I've known it since the day we met."

It was true. Scott was protective of his relationship with Harold, and of Harold's bank account. While their bond was undeniable, and Scott did not consider himself a gold digger, he was Harold's lawfully wedded husband and heir to his estate. Money, like blood, attracted sharks. Scott had fended off his share of them during his time with Harold.

Scott was excited to be in Lambertville, and he looked

forward to a trip or two across the river to New Hope. He had kept in touch with a few old friends on Facebook, though he had never considered any of them especially close. He didn't really have close friends except for Harold. Keeping distance was his nature, just as it was his nature to be suspicious. He knew Harold's fondness for drugs, specifically cocaine, could easily mix with his desire for young men into a dangerous cocktail. Nothing too unfortunate had happened yet — unless you considered Scott coming home to find Harold partying with three much younger men, all of them semi-naked, to be unfortunate — but it was only a matter of time. Scott worried that one of these days Harold's impaired judgement could put him at the wrong place and time.

Closing a dresser drawer filled with Harold's clothes, Scott said, "I prefer to think of myself as protective, not jealous. You're a wealthy man, Harold ..."

"You would know."

The comment stung Scott, but he ignored it. Harold was not above holding his wealth over Scott's head, as he often did.

"You're also not the most discreet," Scott continued. "Especially with gin and cocaine in you. Then I really have to stay alert."

"Did you bring it?"

"That's a rhetorical question," Scott replied. He always brought Harold's supply, carefully maintained in a small silver case with the letters 'H. S.' engraved on it. The case included a razor blade, mirror and a straw.

"May I?" asked Harold.

"Do as you please, you always have. It's in the toiletry bag on the sink."

Harold got up from the chair and went into the bathroom. A moment later, Scott heard the familiar click-click-click of the razor blade against the case's inside mirror. Then a sudden, loud sniff. He both hated it and welcomed it. Harold would be in a good mood now. Harold would be energetic, witty, and as friendly as Harold got. It had been a deal with the Devil throughout their relationship, and Scott worried that someday the Devil would come to collect. He proceeded to put his own clothes in a lower drawer and braced himself for the new and improved Harold who would emerge from the bathroom any moment now.

CHAPTER 8

Kyle was not in the habit of staying in the house once everyone was checked in. He and Danny were the proprietors, not friends of the guests or tour guides. They'd spoken to other B & B owners to learn the ins, outs, dos and don'ts, and had decided before opening the doors they would be as invisible as possible. That meant getting people settled in, showing them the house — including instructions that the rooms on the third floor belonged to Patty and Justin and were off limits to wandering houseguests — then leaving them to enjoy themselves at their leisure. If anything was needed, they could use a house phone installed in the parlor specifically for the purpose of reaching one of the staff: dial #1 for Patty, #2 for Justin, or #3 for Kyle and Danny. Patty had been listed first because she was the most efficient and reliable of the in-house staff. She could be counted on to assess a situation and either handle it herself, or escalate it appropriately. After two months in business, Kyle had only been summoned once, to soothe an angry guest who'd seen a mouse in her room and was under the mistaken impression that a bed and breakfast was the same as a luxury hotel in Manhattan.

Today, however, Kyle decided to linger. Having every room booked, so much *presence* in the house, made him stay around to savor the moment. Along with the two famous writers and their spouses, there was the young couple, Belinda and John Millaman; the second couple, David and Sam Kopeck-Stiller, from Philadelphia; and the quiet elderly gentleman, Joseph Garland, who did not say where he was from, or much at all, except that he'd come to town to research his family history. Ancestry was all the rage now, and the only thing that had seemed unusual to Kyle was how old Garland was. Maybe, Kyle thought, he'd wanted to research his roots while he still had some time to do it.

They had decided early in the venture that Kyle would be the public face of Passion House. After running Margaret's Passion in Gramercy Park for so many years, Danny had had enough contact with customers and guests. He intended to stay in the background and let Kyle deal with people. This excluded breakfast, which they would eat with whatever guests wanted to enjoy Danny's cooking. Other than that, Danny vanished into the background and out of the house.

Kyle was standing in the parlor, taking a last look around, when Scott and Harold came downstairs.

"I hope you found the room to your liking," Kyle said.

"Oh, absolutely," Scott said.

Harold offered a sniff and a shrug.

Scott added, "Ignore him, he's tired."

"We're from here," Harold said. "It's been a few years, though, and I'm curious to see what's changed."

"We're headed out for a walk to see for ourselves."

Just then Gladys and Carol came down the stairs behind them. Gladys gripped the banister, taking the steps in the one-foot-two-foot descent of people for whom steps were not so easy anymore.

Harold glanced up, locking eyes with Gladys for a moment before looking away.

Gladys froze.

"Let's go, then," Harold said. "You have the key?"

Scott pulled the housekey from the pocket of his khakis and waved it at Harold.

"The door's unlocked until ten," Kyle said.

"Harold likes to be prepared," said Scott. "We might get wild and stay out until ten-thirty."

"Aren't you Harold Summit?" Gladys asked, halfway to the first floor.

Standing by the front door, Harold turned to her. "Yes, I am. And you are?"

"She's Gladys Finch," Carol said, as if that should be universally known. "*The* Gladys Finch."

Kyle watched, fascinated, as the egos of two successful writers suddenly came into contact.

"You're here for the conference," Scott said. "I'm assuming."

The conversation had given Gladys and Carol enough time to reach the bottom of the stairs.

"You assume correctly. She's on a *panel*," Carol said, emphasizing the special status it gave Gladys.

"I turned them down," Harold replied, haughtily. "I don't do panels anymore." Turning to Scott, he added, "Let's go now, please, I'm hungry."

"There are plenty of good places to eat in Lambertville," Kyle offered. "Or just walk across the bridge to New Hope."

Harold glared at him. "We're from here. Did we not say that?"

"You did," Kyle stammered. "I was just ..."

"Ignore him," Scott said, saving the moment. "He's irritable, he's hungry ..."

"He's Harold Summit," Gladys finished. "I'm surprised he didn't book the entire place for himself. He can afford it."

Harold's eyes narrowed. "Then you do know me, Ms. Finch."

"Anyone who's ever been to a grocery store knows who you are," Gladys answered. "Your name's on the rack with all the other dime-a-dozen paperbacks."

"Oh," Harold said, "but those dimes add up."

"I'm sure they do," Gladys said. She turned to Kyle, who'd been watching the curious exchange, and asked, "Do you have any coffee, by chance?"

"Certainly," said a voice.

They turned and saw Patty standing by the wide doorway into the dining room. She'd been so quiet no one had noticed her.

"Have a seat, ladies, and I'll bring you fresh coffee. We also have scones and some cookies, if you'd like."

"We'd like that very much," Carol said, ushering Gladys to one of two couches.

"Enjoy yourselves," Harold said. "We really must go."

"Patty, thank you so much," Kyle said, his first words since the exchange between Finch and Summit. "I'll be in the guest house with Danny."

They still called it the guest house even though it was their home and they were not the guests.

Scott and Harold left, closing the door behind them and heading up the walkway. Carol and Gladys made themselves comfortable on the couch while Patty disappeared into the kitchen.

Kyle took a last look around, pondering what he'd just seen and heard. There was something between Harold Summit and Gladys Finch, he was sure of it, but was it just vanity? Professional jealousy?

It was going to be an interesting few days.

CHAPTER 9

"He doesn't remember you," Carol said.

"Of course he does. He knows perfectly well who I am."

Carol had always thought Gladys had an inflated sense of her own importance, but she wouldn't dare say it, and in fact encouraged it. A writer like Gladys would never be wealthy and would have to accept reputation in lieu of significant royalties. Carol believed it was possible that Harold Summit did not remember Gladys. And she believed he may not have intentionally plagiarized Gladys's work, but Gladys believed it to her simmering core, and what Gladys believed was treated as the truth in their household.

After having coffee and cranberry scones, Gladys and Carol had returned to their room. Carol wanted to walk around town and see what Lambertville had to offer, which her online research had told her was a lot. There were several restaurants she was sure Gladys would enjoy, if she could just get her to put on her sneakers and leave. She knew that was going to be a challenge, given Gladys's tendency toward inertia. The only place Gladys gladly went most days was to her computer to write.

Attempting to change the subject, Carol said, "There's a bookstore in town. I know you love a good bookstore."

"Speaking of which, did you notice two of my books on the shelf downstairs?" Gladys asked.

"You're as popular as ever."

"They haven't been read. It was a calculated placement."

Carol sighed, wondering how she would ever get Gladys out of her funk, short of ending Harold Summit's career.

"Why don't you take a nap?" Carol said. "I can go for a stroll and you can get caught up on some sleep."

"You know I love you."

The words surprised Carol. Gladys was as devoted to her as she was to Gladys, but it wasn't the kind of reassurance Gladys offered much. Their commitment to each other had been so long, and so solid, neither expressed it often. Hearing Gladys say it out loud, for no apparent reason, worried Carol. It made her think of people saying "I love you" before they left the house, never to be seen alive again. *Stop it, Carol*, she told herself. *She's just telling you she loves you ... for no reason.*

"I know you do," Carol replied. "And I love you, too. I want you to be rested. We have a conference to attend, and a fabulous town to explore."

"I'm an explorer of the mind," Gladys said. "You don't need sensible walking shoes to go there."

"Fair enough. Now you lie down, read a little bit, take a nap. I'll be back in an hour, I promise."

Gladys nodded and eased herself onto the bed, the only thing in the room she considered comfortable. "If they ask us to review this place, the mural has to go."

"It's probably nostalgia."

"Then it's misplaced, and I'll tell them that. Now go and enjoy yourself. Bring me back something delicious."

Carol walked over to the bed and kissed Gladys on the cheek. Her heart swelled with love at the sight of her wife's face. She knew Gladys had resisted marrying because of her longstanding problems with an institution she saw as oppressive, but she had done it for Carol, and Carol could not be happier. She would bring Gladys something tasty from a local shop. That always lifted Gladys's mood, which was in dire need of improvement.

Carol got her purse from the dresser and quietly left the room, gently closing the door behind her.

Gladys did not sleep.

CHAPTER 10

Kyle hadn't expected to be as affected as he was by the final move, the last trip back from New York. The pleasure he'd imagined at having finally sold the apartment was tempered by the realization that *they had finally sold the apartment.* There was no going back. They still owned the building the restaurant was in. They had income from tenants. They had dealings with the managing agent who ran the building. They would visit the city, perhaps often, but they would never live there again.

"Are you sad?" Kyle asked.

Danny was lying on the couch reading Kirsten's newest mystery, the one they were hosting a signing for the next night.

"Of course," Danny replied. "But this is life, right? We lose our parents—your dad's been gone a long time now—then our siblings, and finally us."

"I wasn't going that far. I just meant about moving."

"Yes and no. I like living here. I was tired of the concrete and the noise."

"And the memories," Kyle said. "Be honest."

It was true. New York City had become the past for them in so many ways. They still had friends there, but those friends could come see them, or Kyle and Danny could drive into the city for a day, but the last year had been about letting it all go.

"Eventually, memories are mostly what we have left," Danny said. "Now please let me read. It's a good book. And Rox Harmony is obviously Detective Linda."

Kyle knew that Linda had not liked being the model for her wife's protagonist, a private detective whose backstory was remarkably similar to hers. But Kirsten had three books out in the series and there were at least two more in the works, from what Linda told them.

Kyle and Linda had solved five murders together, beginning when Kyle and Danny were just names on a list of suspects and Linda was investigating a suspicious death at Pride Lodge. They'd called her Detective Linda ever since, even though she'd retired and wasn't fond of the nickname.

"I wonder if Kirsten's going to the conference," Kyle said, thinking out loud.

"It would make sense. She's a mystery writer."

Kyle had not thought to ask Kirsten about it when they'd visited the women's house the previous week.

"Mostly I hope the reading goes well," Kyle said. "I'd hate to have three people show up."

"I'm sure she's used to these things. And again, please, I'm reading."

"I'll shut up."

Kyle left Danny to his book and the two cats, each perched on an arm of the couch like happy sentinels watching over their human. He went into the kitchen, sat at the table and went over the menu again for tomorrow's breakfast. Danny had planned a vegetable frittata, fruit bowl, bacon on the side for meat eaters, and homemade carrot muffins. Kyle stayed out of Danny's way when he was cooking, working with Patty to set the table and greet the guests as they came out of their rooms. Each of them were asked by Patty ahead of time if they planned to attend so she could get a headcount.

So far, only Joseph Garland said he would not be there. He'd booked his room for a week and was a man of few words. He wasn't unpleasant, just uncommunicative. Kyle had checked him in on Monday and noticed a certain peculiarity about the man. Garland looked to be in his seventies, possibly older, and dressed as if he bought his suits from a 1950s vintage clothing store. And a suit was the only thing he wore. He must have had two or three from the same retailer, in the same design. Kyle had seen him in a gray one, a beige one, and a brown one. White shirts, thin cloth ties, burgundy wingtips, and a black fedora hat he'd tipped at Kyle when he had first shown up at the house. Kyle had tried to make conversation with the man, but Garland had kept his responses short and to-the-point: he was in Lambertville researching the history of the Garland family. Kyle assumed he was like millions of people who'd joined the craze for knowing who their great-great-great-great grandmother was, who she'd had a child with out of wedlock, and where each and every member of their vastly extended family was buried. Personally, Kyle had no interest in knowing where he came from. He knew where he'd grown up, where he'd lived since then, and where he lived now. His father was dead, his mother was remarried and living in Scottsdale, and he'd married the man of his dreams. That was the extent of his interest in a family tree. Garland, however, must have taken it very seriously. The man shuffled off each day to study ... what, exactly, Kyle didn't know. Property records? Cemetery plans? Whatever it was, Joseph Garland didn't say anything about it and Kyle didn't ask. His business was running Passion House, not knowing what other people were up to when they walked out the front door.

Kyle looked forward to having breakfast with the others. He already knew the two couples who'd checked in Monday, taking advantage of the weekday rate, and he'd enjoyed the odd, tense encounter between Gladys Finch and Harold Summit. They had the reading to look forward to, with more people expected in the house than they'd had since opening. It was going to be a busy week, so busy that he might stop thinking about the life they'd left and the memories he could dust off any time he felt like being sentimental.

He took a banana from a bowl on the table, peeled it, and read over the menu one more time.

CHAPTER 11

"She acted like there was something between you," Scott said.

They were strolling along Bridge Street, looking for a coffee shop where Harold could wash down his cocaine with a nice cappuccino. Scott knew Harold would slip into the restroom for another quick snort while he placed their order.

"She's just a jealous author," Harold replied. "I know *of* her, but I don't know her, and I must say I don't want to."

"You'll both be at the conference."

"Along with two hundred other inferior writers. Please change the subject before I regret coming here."

Scott knew things were more complicated for Harold than he would admit. The Connor Dark TV show had been canceled after three episodes, and his most recent book in the series had not sold nearly as well as the first nine. It had also been two years since publication, and Harold spent more time these days surfing the internet than he did writing fiction. Scott had seen Harold's search history many times. He knew Harold's fixation of late was pornography, not research for his new novel, which had been in the outline stage since the last one came out. Harold was not the writer he used to be, a realization that had been eased by an increasing dependence on drugs and gin. The conference was a chance for him to feel important again. His star may have faded, but it was still in the heavens, and enough people would want his autograph and selfies with him to make the trip a bit of a palliative. Scott hoped it would be enough to slow the spiral he saw Harold in. It might even get him to write a chapter or two.

Two blocks from the bridge they came upon the River Brew Coffee Shop. It hadn't been there when Scott lived in the area and it looked inviting, the way a good local coffee shop should. He peered through the window at a long, dark wood counter, a display case filled with muffins and cookies, and several small tables with chairs, two of which were occupied by people enjoying their afternoon doses of caffeine.

"This looks nice," Scott said.

Harold stood behind him, not that interested in the place. "Do they have a bathroom?" he asked.

Scott knew that would be a deciding factor. Once Harold began dipping into his little silver case, he usually kept at it the rest of the day.

"If they don't, we'll just say we're looking and leave. But I'm sure they do. All these places have bathrooms. Did you need to pee?"

"Don't be clever," Harold said.

Facing the window, Scott rolled his eyes.

"I saw that," said Harold. Then, surprisingly, he reached out and patted Scott's butt.

"Your mood has improved," Scott said, while thinking, *Or it's that houseboy, Justin, you're looking forward to.*

Scott opened the door and led the way into the coffee shop. A few minutes later he was sitting at a table picking at a chocolate chip scone, waiting for Harold to come out of the bathroom. *One of these days*, he thought, *he won't come out and they'll find him collapsed on the floor, dead from a heart attack. Or worse, sitting on the toilet, like Judy or Elvis.* He'd been trying for the past six months to convince Harold he needed rehab, to which Harold had replied with firm refusals. Scott knew things might have to get much worse before Harold took the risk to his life seriously. Maybe a mild heart attack would do him good.

He quickly adjusted his expression when he saw Harold come out of the small restroom the coffee shop offered.

Harold took a deep breath, as if inhaling the freshest air imaginable, and winked at Scott. If his mood kept improving, this might be a pleasant trip after all.

CHAPTER 12

Kyle was preparing to run errands in town and had just left the guest house when he saw Joseph Garland walking up the street. The old man was off again on his daily journey to somewhere, destination unknown to anyone but himself.

"Where do you think he goes?" Kyle had asked after Garland had spent his first day and night at the house.

"Well, we know he has at least one friend here," Danny had replied. "They had dinner together."

"So he said. Just like he said he's here researching his family history. But who is he, really? And why is he staying at Passion House?"

Danny had looked at him as if it was a ridiculous question. "We're open for business. Why wouldn't he stay here?"

"It's just odd."

"He's an odd man. People have a right to be strange, Kyle. Stop being so curious. It gets you into trouble."

Kyle watched Garland disappear up the street, then he headed into the house to check in with Patty. When he came through the back door and into the parlor, he saw Patty standing at the big bay window. Had she been watching their peculiar guest go out into the day?

"He's an interesting man," Kyle said.

Patty jumped. He'd surprised her, something that never happened. Patty not only had a way of entering and exiting rooms unseen and unheard, she also had heightened senses that made surprising her almost impossible.

"I try not to wonder too much, Mr. Callahan," she said. "It's not—"

"I know," said Kyle. "It's not your job. You're a valuable asset to anyone who hires you, Patty, that's obvious, and I'm sure discretion is one of your most appreciated skills."

He saw her blush for the first time as she stepped away from the window.

"But still, you have ears, I can see them. And you clean the rooms ..."

It took only a moment for her to realize what he was suggesting.

"Don't look so horrified," Kyle said. "I'm just curious about the man. He could be a jewel thief, or an international criminal hiding out in Lambertville."

"Mr. Durban told me you have quite an imagination," Patty said.

Kyle winced. Had Danny told her about his past? The murderers he'd confronted and brought to justice? The man he'd killed in self-defense? Surely, he thought, Danny would not have told her too much.

"I'm sorry," Kyle said. "I've crossed a line."

"There's no need to apologize. I've wondered about him myself, but it's not my place to ask questions."

Kyle knew she was right. If he wanted to know more about Garland he should just ask the man. But Joseph Garland had already made it clear he was not interested in talking about himself. And asking Patty to spy or eavesdrop, assuming there was anything she could overhear, was improper and unfair.

"Forget I said anything," Kyle said. "Now let's go over my shopping list. We'll need some finger food for the reading tomorrow night, and we're serving wine."

Kyle got a notepad and pen from the kitchen, then came back and sat at the dining table with Patty. They began listing what he'd buy in town, and who would see to which task as they planned for a roomful of guests the following night.

CHAPTER 13

Nighttime had always been Kyle's favorite time of day. He would settle into bed with a book while Danny rested next to him reading a magazine. Leonard would nestle between them and Wilma would stay just outside the bedroom door, staring longingly at the bed but refusing to enter the room.

"She'll come around," Kyle had assured Danny. "It just takes time."

They'd rescued the energetic tortoise shell from a hoarder home. Neither of them knew what the implications of that could be when they'd seen the information on a card above her shelter cage. There were no details about Wilma's situation, just conjecture and speculation once they got her home and realized she had issues: it took two weeks for her to come out from under the couch; she'd fled from Leonard every time he so much as glanced at her; and she remained one of the most skittish cats Kyle had ever met. The best news was that she and Leonard had become good friends, and they imagined it helped Leonard get past the loss of Smelly.

Setting an open novel on his chest, Kyle said, "I saw him coming back tonight."

Danny did not stop reading his magazine, a local publication dedicated to the pleasures of living in the Delaware River Valley. "Who are you talking about?"

"Joseph Garland."

Danny glanced at him. "Oh for godsake, stop thinking about him. Or just ask him what he's up to."

"I know what he's up to! He's researching his family history ... so he says."

"You have a suspicious mind. Most of the time people are exactly who they say they are."

"Most of the time. What if he's a Nazi war criminal?"

"He's too young for that. And he's too old to be a serial killer. I can't see him overpowering anything bigger than a houseplant. It doesn't matter. Whatever he is, he's harmless."

Kyle knew he would not return to his book, so he slipped a

bookmark into it and set it on his nightstand.

"I asked Patty to keep an eye on him."

That got Danny's attention. He looked over from the magazine. "Are you serious? You asked her to spy on him?"

"In so many words, but she wasn't having it. And then she said something interesting."

Danny waited. "Yes?"

"She said you told her I have quite an imagination."

"It's true, Kyle. Exhibit number one is this conversation. We have a guest who clearly wants to be left alone. He's unusual, he keeps to himself, and as far as I can tell he wants nothing more than to go about his business, whatever that is. I'm telling you to respect his wishes. He'll be gone Monday, and then we can get some more guests for you to fantasize about."

"I'm not *fantasizing* about anyone!"

Danny closed his magazine and dropped it to the floor.

"You miss the action, be honest."

"What action?"

"Let's see ... there were the murders at Pride Lodge, the psychopath who almost killed your friend Katherine, Diedrich Keller and his basement of horrors, and Vivian LaGrange. I'm surprised you don't have a shrine to each of them."

The comment, while not spoken harshly, felt like a blow to Kyle. It also felt like the truth. Kyle had thought—had wanted to believe—he'd left his need for the hunt behind him, in a therapist's office on the Upper West Side. He'd ended a man's life, however justifiably, and it had taken months of private sessions to free himself from the guilt. By the time they'd decided to move to Lambertville it had been three years since he'd last been on the trail of a killer, a trail he swore he didn't miss and to which he would never return.

"You're right," Kyle admitted. "Maybe I should call Peter," he added, referring to the therapist he hadn't seen since their last session.

"There are therapists in New Jersey, if that's what you need," said Danny. "I think Peter is the past, as much as I like him and appreciate what he did for you. Let's keep moving forward."

Kyle reached over the patted Danny's hand. "Absolutely," he said. "Forward."

Danny took the TV remote from the headboard shelf behind

them and raised the volume. They put it on mute when they read, then went back to listening when it was time to sleep. Kyle had his favorite shows—the ones he could fall asleep to—and he turned off his nightstand lamp as he listened to the familiar voices from a favorite sitcom in reruns. He began to drift away to the sounds of a laugh track and lines he'd heard a hundred times.

CHAPTER 14

Kyle and Danny looked forward to breakfast. It was the one time they were always in the house, starting the morning off with their guests and enjoying a simple meal Danny prepared with gusto. Some bed and breakfasts offered a modest basket of muffins and an urn of coffee, with the proprietors nowhere to be found. Danny didn't want that, and he had insisted he would make a real breakfast, with everyone together in the dining room around a large table they'd purchased for that purpose. Guests were on their own after that. Kyle and Danny often didn't see them again until the next morning, but they would begin their day at Passion House with conversation and good food.

Danny enjoyed working in the kitchen, with Patty helping out most days. Kyle set the table and made sure everything looked good. They used nice plates and silverware Danny's mother had left them when she and his father moved to Fort Lauderdale. It reminded him of them: his mother had always used "the good china" when she set the table for their weekly Sunday dinners, even though it was neither china nor especially good. It was the sentiment that mattered.

Justin was put to use making sure the house was tidy, taking over the role while Patty assisted in the kitchen.

Guests were served to order once everyone was at the table. Danny kept two skillets ready for eggs, another for hash browns and a third for bacon. Biscuits were baked in the oven. Patty squeezed fresh oranges, and guests were offered their choice between orange or tomato juice. Finally, there was a large toaster they'd picked up at a flea market that could handle eight slices of bread.

Today they would be joined by everyone except Joseph Garland. He had not had breakfast with them any day he'd been in the house, contributing to his air of mystery.

The Kopeck-Stillers were first to arrive. David and Sam had driven to Lambertville from Philadelphia. Both men were in their fifties and, to Danny's pleasant surprise, had once eaten at Margaret's Passion on a trip to Manhattan. They'd been together since college and acted as if they'd been in love every day since. Sam doted on David, who sometimes feigned annoyance at the attention he clearly enjoyed.

Belinda and John Milliman came to the table soon after. They'd been to a destination wedding for Belinda's sister at the Black Bass Hotel, located in Pennsylvania along the river, and had wanted to stay in the area a few days.

Gladys and Carol showed up as Patty was putting pitchers of juice on the table. And no sooner had they taken their seats than Harold and Scott came down the stairs. A few moments later Danny was ready to serve.

Kyle told the group, "We have biscuits, gravy, bacon, toast for those who prefer it, juice, as you can see, and eggs to order. How does everyone want their eggs?"

Kyle made a mental note of each guest's preference and returned to the kitchen, where Danny was at the ready with a skillet and a spatula. Patty quickly filled plates and bowls with the other menu items. Soon everyone had been served and Danny, Kyle and Justin joined them at the table.

The guests had introduced themselves and were enjoying conversation among strangers. It reminded Kyle of the cruises they took where they often found themselves eating with people they'd never met. He always enjoyed hearing their stories and listening as they got to know each other.

"I love the Black Bass," Scott said to the Millimans. "Harold took me there on our second date."

"You're from the area?" asked Belinda.

"It's been a few years. Harold was visiting from Los Angeles, where we live now."

"The answer is yes," Harold said. He was no warmer this morning than he'd been the day before.

"You were here a long time before that, weren't you?" asked Gladys, making it sound more like an accusation than a question.

Harold stared at her. "Yes, most of my life," he replied.

"Before you became famous."

Belinda's eyes widened. "Are you an actor?"

Harold sighed. "No, young lady. I'm an author."

"Gladys is, too," Carol said, proudly and a little defensively. "She's on a panel at the conference."

Harold's eye roll did not go unnoticed.

"You even edited a literary magazine some years ago," Gladys said. It was her turn to stare.

Kyle was fascinated by the interaction as he watched the two literary titans and tried to decode the unspoken messages they were sending each other. Their mutual dislike was evident, and he had the distinct impression there was bad blood between them.

Scott, his head tilted slightly in curiosity, asked Harold, "A magazine? I didn't know that."

"It's nothing," Harold said. "Can we please change the subject? We're not the only ones at this table. In fact, I think I'll get some more coffee. You all just keep talking."

Seeing Harold get up from the table with his coffee cup, Justin quickly said, "I'll show you where everything is," and pushed his chair out.

"It's a coffee pot," Scott said. "I think he can find it."

Ignoring him, Justin said, "There's creamer in the refrigerator, and several kinds of sweetener. I'll help you."

"I'll get it for you," Scott said, jumping up.

"Stay," Harold replied, speaking it as a command. Scott slumped back into his chair, watching as Harold and Justin disappeared into the kitchen.

"So ... " Kyle said, wanting to ease the peculiar tension at the table. "David and Sam, tell us about yourselves."

A moment later the Kopeck-Stillers were talking about their life in Philadelphia and their trip to Lambertville, which was an anniversary present from David to Sam.

"Every few months one of us plans a trip and the other doesn't know where we're going," David said.

"It's a surprise," Sam explained. "We've been doing this for years. It's a way of keeping things interesting in the relationship."

"Oh, I like that," Belinda said. Turning to her husband, she added, "We should try it."

Kyle looked at the kitchen door. Harold and Justin were taking a little long to get a cup of coffee and he wondered what the men might be talking about. He noticed Patty across the table glaring toward the kitchen, silent and disapproving of whatever she imagined was going on by the stove. He hoped Justin was not breaking the house rules and flirting with the man. He made a note to keep an eye on it.

Scott, too, was keeping an eye on it. His back was to the

kitchen door but he'd turned his head slightly, trying to hear whatever conversation was taking place behind him.

Harold and Justin returned. Harold was smiling and carrying a full coffee cup, his mood greatly improved. They sat back down and the breakfast continued as if nothing had happened. But Kyle knew it had, and Scott knew it, too.

CHAPTER 15

"That was weird," Kyle said. "I think Justin is breaking the rules."

They'd returned to the guest house, leaving Patty and Justin to clean up as the others went back to to their rooms or departed for the day.

"Or he's about to," said Danny. "Should we remind him what they are?"

They'd been clear with Justin that fraternizing with guests was not acceptable. It was a polite way of saying he was not to have sex with them. He'd adhered to the prohibition so far, but they had not had a guest as rich and famous as Harold Summit.

"I think we should wait and see," Kyle said. "Maybe Justin was showing him around the kitchen."

"It's a big kitchen," Danny replied, sarcastically.

Danny enjoyed being finished with breakfast almost as much as he enjoyed making it. They were free from the guests for the rest of the day. He'd always been a people person — it was part of running a restaurant — but he'd had enough, and operating a bed and breakfast gave him a balance he liked. Once they finished their morning in the house they were free to do as they pleased. For Danny that meant lunch today with their friend Maggie Dahl, whose jams and jellies everyone had sampled at breakfast. Kyle had been invited but had passed, wanting some free time of his own.

"I won't say anything to Justin," Kyle said. "The last thing I want to do is accuse him of something he hasn't done."

"I don't think he's the one you need to worry about. There's something predatory about Harold Summit. And arrogant."

"You noticed."

Summit had made his superiority complex clear from the moment he'd arrived. He'd sniffed his way around the house, as if it wasn't much better than the cheaper hotels he'd stayed in. He'd barely touched his breakfast, as if that, too, did not meet his standards. And there was the awkward, limited interaction with Gladys Finch that had flared again while they were at the table. Harold did not like Gladys, and Gladys loathed Harold.

"Tell Maggie I said hello," Kyle said. "The invitation for her son and his husband still stands anytime they want to come."

Danny smiled. "If everyone you've offered a free room to showed up, we'd go out of business."

"What else is owning a bed and breakfast good for?"

"It's how we make a living now, Kyle."

Danny got up from the table. Wilma and Leonard were curled up together by a heating vent beneath mounted shelves that held pots and pans. They'd worried the much older Leonard would not take to the feisty newcomer.

"Best buddies," Danny said, nodding at the sleeping cats.

Kyle gave Danny a kiss and saw him out the door. It was a rare morning with no plans, and he wanted to take a long walk along the canal in Lambertville. He and Danny both enjoyed strolling the dirt path next to the canal that ran through town, and that had once brought trains to the area. The tracks were long gone, though there was a section of abandoned rail cars that had been decorated with graffiti by local kids with spray paint and nothing better to do. It was one of Kyle's favorite walks, and a perfect day to go there.

CHAPTER 16

Scott was unhappy. What should have been his triumphant return to town as the husband of a successful author, as a man who would never again have to slice deli ham for anyone, had quickly become a trip he regretted.

"I don't want you at the conference," Harold said. "What would you do there?"

Harold was primping more than usual, which was always a lot. He couldn't hide his age, but he could de-gray his hair, trim his ear and nose hair, spritz himself with cologne, and wear something more tight fitting than a man his age ought to wear.

"Not so heavy on the Aramis," Scott said from the bed. He was lying propped up on pillows, his arms crossed over his chest, his fingers fidgeting. "It makes people choke when you walk by."

Harold glared at him in the mirror. "Stop pouting," he said.

This was not the first time Harold had left him alone while he attended a conference or function. Had Scott not known better, he would have thought Harold was ashamed of him. He knew Harold had never officially come out and had yet to dedicate a book to his husband.

"Everyone knows you're gay," Scott said.

"I don't make a secret of it. I'm just discreet. My readers—"

"Your readers don't care who you sleep with," Scott interrupted. "Those days are long gone, Harold. Nobody gives a shit. And as for being discreet, you weren't this morning."

Scott's mood had dropped precipitously since breakfast. He'd noticed how much time Harold had spent in the kitchen with Justin and could only imagine what had been arranged.

"I asked the young man what was new in Lambertville," Harold said unconvincingly. "We got lost in conversation, that's all."

"Whatever you say, my love."

Harold ignored him, finishing up at the dresser. He opened the top drawer, took out his sleek, silver case and slipped it into his pocket.

"Be careful with that," Scott said. "Cocaine is still illegal."

Harold walked over to the bed, leaned down and kissed Scott on the forehead. "I wish you would trust me."

"I wish you would be trustworthy."

"We're married, Scott. I am, as you clearly think, an old man. I have no interest in finding anyone else, even if I had the time left on this planet it would take to meet them. I love you."

"And I love you," Scott said, managing to relax a little. "I just ... worry about you. People can have designs on men like you."

Harold said nothing, smiling at Scott.

Realizing he may have just described himself, Scott quickly said, "Go then, have a wonderful time. Watch out for a knife in the back from Gladys Finch. She hates you for some reason."

Harold waved his concern away. "Petty jealousy, professional envy. It comes with success."

"And success requires another book. Less time snorting, more time writing."

"I'm working on it," Harold replied. "Now have a lovely day and I'll see you for lunch."

Harold's one concession to Scott's displeasure was to agree to have lunch at Bernadette's, a restaurant on Union Street that hadn't been there when they were last in town. They'd seen it on their stroll the previous afternoon and thought it looked like a good place to eat.

"Twelve-thirty," Scott said. "I'll get us a table."

Harold leaned down again, kissing Scott a second time. "You worry too much," he said.

A moment later Harold was gone, leaving Scott to imagine a conference he would not be at, encounters he would not overhear, and a tryst with a houseboy he hoped never happened.

CHAPTER 17

"You plan to do *what*?" Carol asked, startled.

The women had gone back to their room after breakfast. Both had enjoyed what Danny offered, leaving empty plates for Patty to gather as they left the table. Gladys had been quietly fuming since they'd first encountered Harold in the parlor the day before. Carol knew her anger was heading toward a boil, and did not want Gladys damaging her own reputation for the sake of revealing what one of America's more successful writers had done to her.

"I'm going to expose him during the panel," Gladys said.

"Quietly," Carol replied. "That was the plan, to get him aside and tell him you knew exactly what he did, not shout at him in front of a room full of people. It won't look good."

"I don't care how it looks. I'm seventy-two years old. Do you really think I'm concerned at this point what anyone thinks of me? I don't even *write* mysteries! I joined this stupid alliance for one purpose only, and this is that purpose."

Gladys was sitting in one of the chairs, rubbing her feet. She'd gotten steadily wider over the last few years. She wasn't ready to start using a scooter—something she'd asked Carol to euthanize her for if it ever came to that—but her knees had needed replacing several years ago, and her hips were close behind. Just walking back up the stairs had taken a toll on her.

Carol was at the closet, deciding what clothes to lay out for Gladys. She took a denim jumper out and laid it on the bed. Normally, Gladys preferred pants, but they were too constricting on her failing legs.

Speaking in a serious tone that was unusual for her, and avoiding Gladys's eyes, Carol said, "You want to go out on top, don't you, sweetheart?"

Gladys stopped rubbing her feet. "What's that supposed to mean?"

Carol took a large, long-sleeved red T-shirt from the dresser and laid it next to the jumper. "You're a legend. Why risk tarnishing that by making a scene everyone is going to talk about?"

"*Because* everyone is going to talk about it!" Gladys snapped. "He stole my story, Carol. He took Connie Dark, my creation, and turned it into Connor Dark, a very lucrative franchise that has him living in luxury while we had to scrape the money together just to get here. No, Carol, this is my stand to make, and I'm making it."

Carol blushed, still not looking at Gladys. She knew her wife was right. Gladys had been deprived of the money and recognition that came with the kind of success Harold Summit enjoyed from a character he'd first encountered in her short story almost twenty years ago. Gladys had been well established by then, but she'd wanted to stretch, to try something new. She'd sent the story, a mystery/thriller, to a small literary magazine in New Jersey. The editor of that magazine had been Harold Summit. The reply had been dismissive, prompting Gladys to shred the story, keeping not so much as an outline in her possession. Several years later the first Connor Dark thriller hit the bookstores, and Harold was on his way to becoming a wealthy man. Gladys could have accused him of plagiarism then, or at any time over the ensuing years, as one Connor Dark novel after another came out, increasing Harold's wealth and fame each time. But she had no proof, no way of convincing a court that the series was in fact based on a character she'd created, with a gender change and a different biography.

She's gotten the story back with its cruel rejection letter and promptly deleted it from her hard drive, from her floppy disk, from everywhere it could possibly be. That's how devastated and embarrassed she'd been. She was Gladys Finch, an icon. She was established and sought-after as a godmother of lesbian literature. Bad short stories in a genre she'd never tried before or since would not do. She'd washed her hands of mysteries, and of Connie Dark, until she saw Harold Summit's first novel at the bookstore. She had tried to forget it, to chalk it up as the price she'd paid for being hasty and self-doubting. She'd told a few people here and there that the wildly successful series was based on a character she'd created, a character stolen from her, but with no way to make the accusation stick, she'd let it settle down deep inside her, burning through her like acid. She'd become a secret stalker of the man who'd robbed her, obsessively tracking him online. Then she'd seen on his website that he was attending the

Mystery Authors Alliance conference, and she'd decided to confront him at last. She would let the world know that Harold Summit was a thief.

"Be prepared," Carol said softly, having finished putting Gladys's clothes on the bed.

"For what?" asked Gladys.

Carol shrugged. "I'm not sure, but things will change after this. Some people will believe you, some people won't."

"I don't care."

"I know that. But it's a serious accusation. He could sue you."

"And get what, Carol? All the money I never made from a character he stole from me?"

"I'm just saying."

"Well, stop saying. Let's get dressed and get out of here."

"Yes, sweetheart."

"Calling me 'sweetheart' isn't going to make me less angry."

Carol winced.

Gladys placed a hand on each arm of the chair and hoisted herself up. Feeling guilty for lashing out at Carol, she said, "I love you, you know that. I just need you to support me on this. It may be the last big splash I make."

Carol nodded, saying nothing, as Gladys headed into the bathroom to shower.

CHAPTER 18

Kyle never tired of walking in Lambertville, strolling several times a week along Union Street, then up and down the side streets, and often across the bridge to Pennsylvania. Danny sometimes went with him, but just as often Kyle went by himself. While they were not retired, the option of spending all their time together became a real possibility with Passion House and they'd decided early on to avoid that.

Kyle's first stop before heading out was a quick check of the house. He knew the guests would be gone or leaving, and he liked to see if Patty needed anything for the day. There was also the book reading that night and he wanted it to go smoothly. He'd made a note to himself to call Linda and Kirsten later that morning, to make sure everything was set on their end. They would use the parlor for the reading, and the dining room table for Kirsten to sign books afterward. Justin had been tasked with getting some additional folding chairs from a local church that used them for AA meetings, taking Kyle and Danny's car to bring them over.

"Where's Justin?" Kyle asked, seeing that the dining table was back to its normal state and the kitchen had been cleaned.

Patty was dusting the parlor furniture, keeping the house almost neurotically spotless.

"He went to the hardware store," she said. "To get a washer for the kitchen sink. It's been spraying water."

"I hadn't noticed."

Patty smiled at him, the patient smile she offered people she considered less conscious of their surroundings, which was everyone. Kyle knew she believed it was her duty to be aware of errant water leaks and toilet stoppages.

"Well," said Kyle, "tell him to see me when he needs the car keys. I'm happy to go with him to get the chairs."

"I'll let him know, Mister Callahan."

Kyle looked at her. "Will you ever just call me Kyle?"

"That's not likely."

"Someday you're going to cut loose, Patty, I know you will.

You'll start calling us by our first names, and the next thing you know we'll find you dancing on the porch while you water the plants. I see it coming."

"That's not likely," she repeated, then she returned to her dusting.

Kyle left the house and walked toward town.

Kyle had never fancied himself a small town boy. He'd grown up in Chicago, moved to New York City to pursue David, his first love, and had expected to be an old man riding the subway and walking a few blocks to the nearest senior center. He knew Danny had thought the same thing. They were New Yorkers through and through, and had it not been for their trips to Pride Lodge, outside New Hope, they probably would have stayed that way. They'd wanted a getaway from the city eight years ago, somewhere that didn't require air travel or a long car drive. Kyle became friends with Teddy Pembroke, the handyman who worked there at the time, and it was Teddy's mysterious death, his body found fully clothed and broken at the bottom of the empty swimming pool, that had brought then-detective Linda Sikorsky into their lives. Years later, Kyle reflected on the serendipity of it: It had brought them to New Hope and Lambertville, and to this new phase of their journey. He loved living in a small town with restaurants, art galleries, friendly people, and the extraordinary natural beauty of the Delaware River Valley. He had no regrets.

He'd turned right from Union Street onto Bridge Street when he began to see a few people wearing lanyards and walking toward Lambertville Station. He knew immediately they were conferees in town for the writers convention. He assumed some of them were staying at the Station and had come out for breakfast or to explore the town. He'd decided to stop for coffee at the Brightside Diner, a favorite hangout for locals.

Kyle was a half block from the diner when he spotted Harold Summit walking up the street. He thought about calling out to him, to say hello and ask him if he was enjoying his stay at Passion House, when Harold suddenly turned left at the canal.

That's odd, thought Kyle. He expected Summit to follow the others and head up to the conference. He remembered that Harold was from the area and would know where he was going —

wherever that was.

Built in the 1830s, The Delaware and Raritan Canal once provided an easy means of transportation for freight between Philadelphia and New York, allowing shippers to trim significant miles and time off their trips. Lambertville Station had been just that: a train station. The canal itself, even for those unfamiliar with it, had clearly had railroad tracks on its banks. It was one of the charms of the area, and Kyle had fantasized what it must have been like in the days when locomotives stopped in town to drop off goods and people.

He considered trying to catch up with Summit, then thought better of it. Something told him the man may want to be alone, or possibly on his way to meet someone. He struggled with the idea of following him, to satisfy his curiosity. Instead, he watched Harold Summit disappear up the path, then he made his way to the diner.

It's not your concern, Kyle told himself. *Remember what prying into other people's lives got you. Serial killers. Murderers. Therapy.* Things he had left behind in New York City and did not want moving to Lambertville with him. Harold Summit was a free man. What he was doing on a detour along the canal was none of Kyle's business.

Kyle got to the diner, opened the door, and stepped inside to the sight of familiar faces. It was time for coffee and a newspaper.

CHAPTER 19

It wasn't Justin's first trip to the railroad cars. Everyone in the area who walked along the canal knew they were there. Kids had covered the old, rusting hulks with spray paint, leaving signs of their existence in colorful nicknames and primitive artwork. The insides of the cars were filthy, littered with beer cans and condoms. Justin had climbed inside only once, and that had been enough. Getting into the cars was risky and could easily lead to a bad cut or a sprained ankle. If he met someone there for sex or to buy a bag of weed, he met them outside, just off the trail. That's where he waited this morning, lingering as if he were taking pictures of the railcars.

The trail wasn't busy today. It was a weekday, and the few walkers he'd encountered were locals who regularly strolled the path. Some he recognized, including one middle-aged woman with a dog named Betty. He waved hello but avoided conversation. He wasn't here for that. He'd come at considerable risk to meet a houseguest.

Justin was nervous. He had no doubt Kyle and Danny would fire him if they knew what he was doing. He'd tried to resist the temptation Harold Summit presented to him, but his sex drive was something almost beyond his control. He'd been engaging in casual sex—*enjoying* was not the word, since it was often more of a mechanical urge than something he took any great pleasure in— since he was thirteen. And while he'd matured in many ways, giving up excessive drinking, pills, and more than the occasional joint, he had been unable to control his craving for men.

He looked at his watch. He'd left the house a half hour ago, telling Patty he needed to get some things at the hardware store. The kitchen sink had conveniently begun leaking, once he'd removed the washer inside the faucet head. He didn't really need a reason to go out, but he hadn't felt like making up an excuse. Patty was nosy. Patty watched him, like she watched everyone in the house. She didn't act so much like a mother as like a busybody aunt, and he wanted to be able to give her a receipt from the store. He would replace the missing washer with the new one he'd bought, and no one would be the wiser.

His impatience was becoming unbearable. He'd been gone too long, and now he'd have to invent something to explain why his simple errand took this much time. He was thinking of picking up some scones for the house and a cappuccino, to make his absence more plausible, when he saw Harold walking toward him on the path. They would not have sex there, of course. They'd agreed to meet away from prying eyes and overly observant housekeepers so they could plan something else, something that gave them more time together. Harold was a rich man. He could easily book a room anywhere.

Justin wasn't after money. It was the attention that mattered, the lust for him that thrilled him, and Harold had been ripe with it. There was also something commanding about the man. When he'd made his interest known, it was as if Justin had found himself in the pull of a tractor beam, unable to break free even if he'd wanted to.

He waved at Harold. Harold waved back.

He felt a tingling in his body, a spreading warmth. This was going to be fun.

CHAPTER 20

"Pretty swanky place," Carol said, looking around the lobby of the Lambertville Station Inn. The property, with its hotel, restaurant and conference center, was housed in a restored nineteenth-century train depot and had done its best to match the perceived grandeur of a bygone era while being modern and exceptionally comfortable. The Inn offered a mere forty-seven rooms, which meant most of the conferees were staying elsewhere. The lobby was small but elegant, with a crisp front desk staff used to steering people to what they called the ballroom.

"Fancy place, fancy price," Gladys replied. Her mood had not improved on the drive over from Passion House. Carol had wanted to walk since it wasn't that far—nothing was very far in Lambertville—but Gladys had been using her failing knees and hips as a reason not to walk much for several years now. Today was no exception, so they'd taken the car and driven less than a mile.

"Just enjoy it," Carol suggested. "We don't travel a lot anymore."

"Thank Goddess."

They'd mingled with other arriving attendees for several minutes before heading to the spacious conference room where the Mystery Authors Alliance was holding its gathering. Once they got to the room they registered with a pleasant but harried young woman sitting at a table where name tags had been carefully arranged in neat rows.

"Finch," Gladys repeated, annoyed at not having her name immediately recognized. "F-I-N-C-H."

The woman became flustered, scanning her list on a clipboard, then running her finger along the alphabetical name tags.

"I can't seem to find ..."

"Gladys Fucking Finch. I'm on a panel in twenty minutes. I was invited to be."

"Yes, of course," the woman said. She glanced at the empty

chair next to her, vacated by her counterpart who'd taken a quick bathroom break.

"Here it is," Carol chirped, finding their name tags halfway down a row. "Everything's fine." Looking at the woman's name pinned to her blouse, she added, "Louise, thank you for being so helpful."

Gladys snatched her tag from Carol and marched into the room. "I need to sit down," she said.

Watching Gladys trudge into the conference room, Carol said to the young woman, "Thank you, really, you're doing a great job."

The woman looked about to cry.

The panel was scheduled for 11:00 a.m., the second session of the day. Gladys was relieved. She didn't want to spend any more time at the conference than she had to, and she'd planned to deliver her fireworks and be gone by noon. She had rehearsed her speech for weeks and was mumbling it to herself while Carol was off getting coffee and mini-muffins from a long table against the wall.

For many of us, plagiarism ought to be a capital offense. It first offends the one from whom the plagiarized material was stolen, does it not? Left undiscovered, it lessens them, and in my case, it prevented a future that could have been. A lucrative future of multiple-book deals and movie rights. A future that was rightfully mine ... had not Harold Summit plundered my ideas. You've seen his books on the bestseller lists, you've read about his rise to fame and fortune. You may even know him personally, but what you did not know until today is that his empire was built on a lie, a theft. Connor Dark was my invention, re-gendered, turned into a heterosexual antihero and marketed with spectacular success. I'm here this morning to tell the world that success is founded on a fraud.

She had imagined the reaction, the gasps, as a room of authors turned to stare at Harold Summit and watch his face redden in humiliation. He would deny it, of course. He would protest, possibly right there in the room. He may even storm out in an act of feigned indignation, but the truth would be told, the damage done. She couldn't prove he'd stolen her story because the proof no longer existed, but it didn't matter. Justice would be served.

"Are you okay, sweetheart?" Carol asked. She was standing over Gladys, having set a cup of coffee and a small plate of muffins on the table. "You look upset."

"I'm fine," Gladys replied, smiling up at her. "I was just enjoying myself for a moment."

"Excellent. I knew you'd have a good time once we got here."

"Oh," said Gladys, "I'm going to have a very good time."

Unfortunately for Gladys, Harold Summit never showed up.

CHAPTER 21

Scott had been sitting at a window table at Bernadette's for twenty minutes. The popular restaurant had not been in business the last time he was in Lambertville. Some of the town had changed, but much had stayed the same. Retailers came and went, but he was relieved to see Bridge Street was not dotted with empty storefronts, which had been the fate of so many small towns.

He'd left the bed and breakfast late morning after relaxing in the room with a book. He hadn't been much of a reader before he met Harold, but he'd discovered that he enjoyed getting lost in a good story. His preferred subject was romance, something Harold derided as beneath the mind of anyone who had one. He especially liked the genre called MM romance, in which men fell in love with each other and a happy ending was obligatory. Scott wanted a happy ending ... and not the kind he worried Harold was planning to have with Justin.

The waitress returned to his table, asking if he'd like a refill on his coffee. It would be his third cup since sitting down, and he waved her away. He didn't like taking up a table when all the others were occupied, but he expected to be having lunch with Harold any minute now.

Where is he? he wondered, glancing at his watch again.

He regretted not insisting on accompanying Harold to the conference. He never had before, but there was a first for everything. It was high time Harold stopped hiding himself and his marriage from people. "We're legal now," he'd told Harold many times. "Respectable, even."

"I'm from a different time," Harold had said. It was an excuse he'd often used when confronted with the complications of a new era.

"That's the past," said Scott. "I'm the present. *We're* the present."

"I'll lose readers."

It was Harold's common justification for staying professionally closeted.

Scott had sighed. He refused to believe more than a handful

70

of fans of the Connor Dark series would stop reading the books if they knew the author was a married gay man.

"You're ashamed of me," Scott said the last time it had come up.

"I'm not ashamed of you."

"Then ashamed of *yourself.*"

Harold had glared at him. "I don't carry banners," he'd said. "I don't do causes."

"Being free is not a cause."

Harold had stopped talking then and had not spoken to Scott for two days. It had been among an increasing number of cold spells between them, and it had made Scott think of their prenuptial agreement, a contract that would be voided only if Scott was a widower, not a divorcee. He had not brought it up again. He'd worried Harold was growing distant, and at the same time less cautious. Harold's cocaine use had gotten worse, as had his flirting and the long drives he took once or twice a week. Harold explained them as a way to clear his head, or to think about his next book. But Scott suspected they were meant to give Harold time away from him, and with other men. It wasn't hard to find them anymore. All it took was an app on a smartphone, which might explain why Harold guarded his so closely.

Scott started to see people from the conference strolling down the street outside. He could tell by the lanyards hanging around their necks. He looked at his watch. Harold was now almost a half hour late. He'd tried calling him, but the calls went to voicemail. He hadn't bothered texting. Harold was notorious for not replying and then saying he hadn't seen the message.

Worry was setting in now. What if Harold had tripped and fallen, or had some kind of medical emergency? He waved at the waitress for his check as he pulled his wallet out of his front pocket. He would have to go looking for Harold and hope he didn't regret what he found.

He'd put two dollars down on the table, a generous tip for a cup of coffee and the time he'd taken up at a table for two, when Harold walked into view. Scott felt an immediate sense of relief as he waved Harold into the restaurant.

"I had no intention of attending that panel," Harold said.

The waitress had brought menus, maintaining a professional detachment. She'd offered one to each of them and taken Harold's order for a glass of tomato juice with a side of ice, promising to return in a few minutes after they'd decided their lunch choices.

"You didn't go to any of it?" Scott asked, incredulous. Harold was wealthy, but not one to spend money for which he got nothing. Paying for a three day conference he wasn't attending would normally set Harold off on a lecture about the value of a dollar.

"I knew she was speaking, and I have no interest in what she has to say."

Scott's suspicion that there was bad blood between Gladys Finch and Harold became a certainty.

"What happened between you?" Scott asked.

"Nothing," Harold insisted. "I don't know the woman. I just know I don't like her. And really, Scott, I'm a successful writer. Do you honestly think there's anything for me to learn from someone like her?"

"What does that mean, 'someone like her?'"

"Jealous, angry, probably a man-hater."

"Your misogyny is showing."

"I'm not a misogynist!" Harold said sharply, unaware that the waitress had come back and was standing at the table. Seeing her, Harold looked up and said, "I'm really not, Miss ...?"

"Susan," the waitress said. "And there's no 'Miss.' Just Susan. What would you like today?"

Harold ordered something called a Lambertville Wrap, with a side salad instead of fries. Scott went with a tuna melt, holding his hand over his coffee cup and telling Susan a refill wasn't necessary. She took the menus and hurried away.

Turning back to Harold, Scott asked, "So where were you all morning?"

Harold focused his attention on his paper napkin, unfolding it and putting it on his lap as if it were fine linen. He kept his eyes averted, a giveaway Scott knew well: Harold was about to lie to him.

"I walked over to New Hope," Harold said.

"For two hours?"

"I don't walk fast, Scott, you know that. And there was a lot to see. Familiar stores closed, new ones opened. I thought about walking up to the Giant—"

"Looking for the next me?" Scott said, trying to be playful and failing at it.

Harold frowned at him. "Please don't be insecure. I would not have married you if I didn't intend to spend the rest of my life with you, which, by the way, isn't all that long at my age. You'll get the money, don't worry."

Scott was suddenly torn between crying and throwing his spoon at Harold. He knew plenty of other people thought he'd married Harold to secure his own retirement, but hearing it from Harold was infuriating and embarrassing.

"Let's change the subject," Scott said. "I assume you're attending the rest of the conference? We came a long way to be here."

"Of course I am. And there's a reception this afternoon, which I hope you'll attend with me."

Scott was shocked. Harold had never invited him to any of the conferences he went to. He'd always had to remain at the hotel or entertain himself while Harold glad-handed his way through a crowd of other writers and fans.

"Will they let me?" Scott asked. He hadn't registered—there was no reason to when he wasn't going to be there.

"I'm Harold Summit, of course they'll let you. I think it's time to introduce my husband to the world."

Now Scott really felt like crying, without throwing any utensils. He'd been waiting for this for five years, first as Harold's manfriend, then as his spouse. Would Harold dedicate his next book to him? Would he thank him for his endless patience and unwavering support?

"Of course I'll be there," Scott said. Then, remembering something, he said, "Oh, wait. The book reading at Passion House is tonight."

"No worries," Harold assured him. "The reception's at five-thirty. The reading's at seven, as I recall. Who is this woman anyway, the one who wrote the book?"

"Kirsten somebody," Scott answered. "A friend of the bed and breakfast owners."

"Do we have to?"

"I said we'd be there. And who knows, it might inspire you to finish your novel. It really is time for a new one."

"And we were having such a nice conversation," Harold said.

Susan brought their plates and set them on the table, asking if they needed anything else. Both men shook their heads.

Using his knife and fork, Harold cut into the flour tortilla concealing his sandwich. "What, exactly, is a Lambertville Wrap?" he asked.

Lost in the euphoria of being invited to the reception, Scott forgot about Harold's whereabouts the past two hours. Maybe he was telling the truth for a change and had simply strolled across the bridge to New Hope, or maybe he'd met someone along the way for a quickie. That was Harold, and Scott knew it. He could take it or leave it, and he wasn't about to walk away.

CHAPTER 22

Harold regretted coming all the way from California for a conference he was only attending to stroke his ego. He'd been stuck on the next Connor Dark novel for over a year, pretending to write when he was really surfing the internet aimlessly, with no destination in mind and no ability to add another paragraph to the book. He'd grown tired of Connor and had decided to kill him off. He wanted to get away from the genre altogether and try his hand at something literary, something to showcase his talent as a wordsmith. Unfortunately, he didn't have a single idea for anything *but* a Connor Dark story, and he'd felt trapped by his own creation for a long time. The TV series had failed. He'd sold the movie rights to the first book and seen nothing come of it. His career had stalled. But he was still Harold Summit, still recognizable and revered by his fans, many of whom were other authors—*lesser* authors—who looked up to him as a kind of beacon of hope. *If Harold Summit could rise to the top, maybe they could, too.* He knew very few of them would, but he'd been happy to take their flattery and the occasional speaking fee to convince them their dreams could come true.

The only thing he'd liked about the trip so far was his brief tête-à-tête with Justin Stritch by the rail cars. Harold had wanted a quickie then and there, but Justin had demurred, saying it was not a suitable location for the passion he intended to unleash once they were in a proper setting. Harold told him he had the use of a friend's condo if he needed it, a bit of information he'd kept from Scott, and the men agreed to meet that night after the book reading.

"How will you get away?" Justin had asked. It was a question he'd have to answer for himself, but it wasn't that unusual for him to go out at night. He was staff at Passion House, not an indentured servant.

"Don't worry your pretty head about it," Harold had replied. "I sometimes take strolls to clear my mind and have a nightcap. Alone. Scott won't care."

Justin knew it was a lie. Scott would care very much, but that was between them, and Justin had decided the state of their marriage was none of his business. As long as Scott didn't know who Harold was having his nightcap with, Justin saw no problem with it.

"I have to get back," Justin had said, glancing down the trail as if someone would see them. "Patty's watching the clock, I know it. She's a nosy one. I made sure to buy some things at the hardware store and get a receipt." He waved his bag at Harold.

Harold had given Justin a hug and watched as he hurried onto the path and headed home, then he'd taken a walk over the bridge to New Hope. He wasn't due to meet Scott for lunch for another hour and he was not in a hurry to get anywhere. He would not sit through a panel with that awful woman bleating nonsense about character creation and the sanctity of authorship, as if people who wrote genre fiction were artists. He'd met too many writers over the years who thought they were Michelangelo with a keyboard. The conference would be full of them, and he'd decided to keep his attendance to a minimum.

He walked into Lambertville Station, admiring its small ornate lobby, and was directed to the ballroom by a cheerful older woman behind the desk. The lunch break was winding down and he saw people standing around talking in an animated fashion near the entrance. Conference goers were like that: laughing too easily and deliberately, waving their arms, or focused over-seriously on topics in which they considered themselves experts. And always the side glances, to make sure they were seen. *Look at me, I'm somebody.* Harold knew these events were as much about exposure and *networking*, a term he loathed, as they were about learning anything they didn't already know. He lifted his shoulders back and took a deep breath, wishing he'd dipped into his little silver case again before he got here. He'd had just a sniff in each nostril in the bathroom at lunch.

He noticed immediately that something was off. Several people from different groups turned and looked at him. *Glared* at him. It wasn't the kind of star-struck gawking he was used to. Then, to his surprise, a few of them pointed at him, leaned into the others they were talking to, and whispered.

His hand quickly went to his fly, brushing it to see if he'd left his zipper open. Had he walked around town and gone to the restaurant exposed? Surely Scott would have noticed and said something.

No, the zipper was closed.

Another person, a short, wide woman with a purple streak in her gray hair, narrowed her eyes at him and said something to the others in her group. All four of them turned and gave him an accusatory look he'd never seen before.

The woman broke away and walked up to him.

"Thief!" she said loudly, causing all of them, in every group, to singe him with their eyes.

"What are you talking about?" Harold asked, stepping back from the force of her anger.

"We know what you did," the woman said. "To Gladys Finch. She told us."

Harold felt his stomach tighten.

"I don't know Gladys Finch," he said.

"You don't have to know a writer to steal from them," said the woman. "How can you live with yourself?"

Trying to sound innocent, a man defending his honor, Harold shot back, "I've never stolen anything from anyone, and I've never had to. I'm Harold Summit! Are you sure you're talking to the right person?"

They were all staring at him now. He glanced past them into the room and saw it: Gladys Finch holding court at a table, surrounded by sympathetic writers. Would they all accuse him now? Would they try to sue him, to extort money, claiming his ideas had been theirs?

"Oh, I'm talking to the right person," the woman said. Her name tag identified her as J.L. Hunnicott, a pseudonym if Harold had ever seen one.

Harold had had enough. He bore his eyes into the woman calling herself J.L. and said, "I don't know Finch, and I don't know you, and we'll keep it that way. Now, if you'll excuse me ..."

He intended to walk past her into the ballroom, making the kind of imperious entrance he was practiced at, but his feet had other ideas. As if having an out-of-body experience, he turned and quickly left the premises, walking out onto the main drive and up toward Bridge Street. He carried the weight of their stares with him. He did not turn around, certain they'd followed him and were gathered in a cluster—a coven—watching him flee the scene.

He patted the pocket of his windbreaker. The silver case was there. He needed it now more than ever, to restore a sense of balance, of the outrage he'd manufactured so quickly. Who did they think they were, these trolls with purple hair and preposterous pennames? He was Harold Summit, a star. They needed him to lend legitimacy to their stupid conferences; he did not need them.

He decided it was time to go home. He'd take a long walk to cool off, to reassure himself that the accusations would not stick and his reputation would remain intact. He would return to Passion House, instruct Scott to pack their bags, and leave. He'd promised his friend Victor, the one whose condo he'd been offered should he need some privacy, they would all have dinner while he was in town. He decided it would be an early going away dinner as they left Lambertville and this dreadful experience behind. As he headed back to the canal to clear his head, he took his phone from his jacket pocket, pulled up Victor in his contacts, and dialed.

"It doesn't take an hour and a half to go to the hardware store."

There was something triumphant in the way Patty said it, holding out the receipt for Kyle to look at. They were in the kitchen setting up a fruit bowl and fresh coffee to be left in the parlor for guests. The receipt's time stamp said 9:30 a.m. and Justin had returned near 11:00 a.m.

"I thought he picked up some scones," Kyle said, not wanting to make an issue out of Justin's prolonged absence from the house.

"The coffee shop is on the way back, perhaps a five minute stop. He went somewhere, Mr. Callahan."

Kyle smiled at her. "Somewhere you hadn't authorized?"

Patty blushed and slipped the receipt into the pocket of her sweater. She would submit it at the end of the week with any other household expenses. "That's not what I meant."

"I think it is, Patty. You've been hard on Justin since the day we opened. Is there something you don't like about him?"

"It's not my place to like or dislike ..."

"We all do, it's only human. But he's an employee. We like him, and so far he hasn't committed any violations, unless you know something."

Patty hesitated, then said, "He flirts. With men."

Kyle laughed, unable to help himself. "Who else would he flirt with? It's his nature. He's young, he has drives. He flirted with me and Danny at first, which is not why we hired him, I must add."

"Of course not."

"Let him be who he is and don't worry about it. So he took a long time to run errands, it's really not important."

"If you say so."

"I do. Now tell me, have you learned anything about our mysterious Joseph Garland? You seem perfectly capable of gathering information when you want it."

Looking insulted, Patty said, "I have not. He's a nice elderly gentleman researching his family history. That's what he says and I have no reason to think otherwise. Why are you interested in him, may I ask?"

"Instinct, Patty. When you've been through what I have, you develop a heightened ..."

"Suspicion?"

"Curiosity. Like you have about Justin's whereabouts."

His humor lost on her, Patty turned and walked out of the kitchen.

The reading was coming up quickly. Patty had run run into town for cookies and more plastic cups, and Kyle had sent Justin out with the car to pick up an extra twenty chairs from the local Methodist church. Despite being agnostic—Kyle had no opinion on the existence of God and left belief or disbelief to the imaginations of others—he'd always found a certain comfort in church. He'd attended Metropolitan Community Church of New York on and off for many years, and its pastor had signed their marriage license. It was enough religion for him.

He'd arranged to borrow the chairs and had invited several people from the congregation. Doing a headcount on his fingers that included a dozen local residents Kirsten had invited, he realized they would have close to thirty people in the house that night. He and Danny had a dozen folding chairs in the basement for emergencies. There was also the regular seating in the parlor, where Kirsten would read from her book.

"Is thirty people a lot?" he'd asked Kirsten when he called her that afternoon to finalize the details.

"For a reading of a small lesbian mystery? I'd say so. And they won't all show up."

"Are you nervous?"

Kirsten McClellan had never struck Kyle as the nervous type until she began writing novels. When she'd run her own real estate agency she'd given the impression of a woman who knew what she wanted and got it, sometimes with simple bluster. But putting her writing out there, being reviewed, having people like or, in some cases, hate what she'd written, had made her hesitant in the beginning. She was coming out again in a way, this time as an author, someone who put her imagination on display and had to learn that not everyone appreciated the things she imagined. Now, after three books, she was much stronger, much less concerned with the occasional troll scolding her publicly for one perceived fault or another in the stories she told.

"I'm always nervous," Kirsten had replied. "Writing is a very naked experience. Imagine yourself with no clothes on in room full of people and you'll get the idea."

It wasn't something Kyle was inclined to imagine. "How's Linda doing?" he'd asked, changing the subject.

After a moment, Kirsten had said, "It's the one year anniversary of her mother's death."

"Oh my gosh, I didn't realize that."

"Why would you? It's okay. She's going to have to go through this for the rest of her life."

Linda's mother had lived in Philadelphia, and Linda had been fiercely devoted to her. Kyle knew the loss of Estelle Sikorsky had taken a toll on her daughter and he'd tried to comfort her within limits. He knew from his own life that grief was deeply personal and not something other people could effectively ease, especially if they tried. Time would help, and there hadn't been much of it yet — a year was nothing.

"I told her she didn't have to come to the reading," Kirsten had said. "The book's dedicated to Estelle. But she wouldn't have it. She's Linda, she's going to plow ahead. And it's good for her, I think. If anyone knows that life goes on, it's her."

"It's all of us," Kyle had said. "Especially at our age. Life goes on, and we just keep moving up in line until it's our turn."

"Sadly true."

"I'll let you go now. I'm sure you have things to do, and I just saw Justin pull into the driveway. We got extra chairs from the church. Patty's making up a nice spread with finger foods and sweets, and we've got a few boxes of wine."

"You're a star, Kyle. I really appreciate this."

"We love you both," Kyle had said. "We wouldn't be in Lambertville if it weren't for you."

"I hope that's a good thing."

"It's a great thing! I'll see you tonight."

"See you. Love to Danny."

They hung up and Kyle hurried to the door, opening it as Justin climbed the front steps with folding chairs under each arm.

CHAPTER 24

Scott looked at his watch as he walked up Lambertville Station's main driveway. Despite having lived in the area most of his life, he'd never been inside the large complex nestled on the banks of the Delaware River. He knew there were rooms for guests and, obviously, conference facilities, but it was the kind of place where people hosted very expensive weddings, or treated their families to costly vacations. He wasn't sure of the architectural style—he wouldn't know Tudor from art deco—but it was massive, if only in contrast to its surroundings.

He was nervous. He'd never been to a writers convention with Harold, or to a reception. He had no idea what to expect. He walked into the lobby and was surprised at how small it was, with a dark wood interior, a raised area with a fireplace for at most a dozen guests to gather, and a front desk with an antique feel to it that conjured images of Humphrey Bogart checking in.

He'd stopped obsessing over Harold's earlier whereabouts. He doubted his husband had spent hours walking to New Hope, but there was nothing he could do about it. Harold was a liar, he knew that. Harold was secretive, he knew that, too. And Harold had a drug problem. Scott had made his peace with all this over their time together. Harold had made no effort to change his ways, and Scott had known early in their relationship that he could take it or leave it, so he'd taken it. He truly loved Harold and expected to spend the rest of their lives together, with Harold's being shorter given their age difference. He also knew he was no great catch, and Harold was a man who did not pursue what he didn't want.

"May I help you?"

Scott had been lost in thought as he'd walked into the lobby. A woman sorting papers behind the desk glanced up when she saw him enter.

"I'm here for the reception," Scott replied.

He felt naked without a name tag, almost an imposter. What if she noticed? What if she asked for proof of registration? He didn't have any. He wasn't supposed to be here. He was a fraud, or at least he felt like one.

"Down the hallway, in the ballroom," the woman said. She nodded across the lobby, where a narrow hallway led into the building.

"Thanks," said Scott, and he hurried off before she could ask any more questions.

A few moments later he was entering the ballroom. He wondered why they called it that. Did they hold actual balls here? Or was it a throwback to a time consistent with the Inn's atmosphere and origins, a time when trains deposited wealthy urbanites making weekend getaways to the country? The conference tables had been cleared and replaced with tall skinny tables suited to canapés and cocktails. No chairs were in sight. Dozens of people mingled with drinks in hand, refilling them at an open bar set up along the back wall. Clusters of people talked excitedly about whatever mattered to them at the moment. Scott assumed it was themselves and their latest writing projects. It was an authors convention, after all.

He'd been worried about being discovered as an event crasher, someone who didn't really belong there, and he was surprised at how little notice anyone gave him when he entered the room. A few people glanced his way, then just as quickly went back to their conversations. He spotted a man who appeared to be overseeing the event, gliding nervously from one group to the next. Scott made his way to a table where the man was talking to several people. He was young, wearing a dark blue sweater vest over a white short-sleeved shirt, khakis and saddle shoes. Scott pegged him as gay, which increased his comfort a millimeter or so. He stood patiently to the side, waiting for an opening in the conversation.

The man, whose name tag identified him as Evan, turned to leave and almost walked into Scott.

"Excuse me," said Evan. He glanced at Scott's chest expecting a name tag, then looked up, confused. "Are you with the Inn?"

"No," Scott said. "I'm here with Harold Summit."

A hush came over the immediate area. At least three tables were within earshot, and when he said Harold's name a dozen people nearby turned and stared at him. *So this is fame*, he thought. *The mere mention of his name ...*

"He's not here," Evan said, with evident distaste.

"You mean he left already?" asked Scott, dumbfounded.

"Hours ago," said a woman from one of the tables.

Scott turned to her. She was a stump with purple hair, and she glared at him as if he were a slug on her shoe.

"But I'm meeting him here," Scott stammered.

"You'll have to go and find him," the woman sneered. "I don't think he's coming back. Thieves aren't welcome."

What is this bitch talking about? Scott wondered. *Harold has to be here. He invited me to this reception. He's a star.*

Seeing Scott's distress, Evan ushered him quickly to the side. He lowered his voice and explained, "There was an incident earlier with Mr. Summit."

"An incident?"

"Accusations of plagiarism were made."

"Plagiarism?"

"It's when someone steals someone else's work."

"I know what it is. Just because I don't have a name tag doesn't mean I'm stupid."

His patience waning, Evan said, "Mr. Summit left for his own good after Gladys Finch informed everyone that he'd stolen her work and made a very good living from it. Are you a friend of his?"

"I'm his husband!" Scott said loudly.

Another hush, more stares.

"Oh, I'm sorry."

"What is there to be sorry about?" Scott had lost any inclination to be polite. "This ridiculous conference, that's what's to be sorry about! No wonder he never invited me to these things."

"You may want to leave," Evan said.

"There's no 'may' about it. I don't know what happened, but Harold Summit is the most generous, loving, kind man I've ever met." Raising his voice so the entire room could hear him, he added, "And the most talented!"

He turned on his heel and hurried out of the room, down the hallway and out of the building. He grabbed his phone from its belt holster and called Harold as he walked quickly back to Bridge Street.

The call went to voicemail.

CHAPTER 25

Kyle was nervous. He'd never had this many people in the house—or any other place he'd lived. He and Danny were not the entertaining types, and even when they'd held parties at their New York apartment they had never invited more than a half-dozen friends. Tonight he saw several times that filing through the front door.

The folding chairs Justin had brought from the church were added to the chairs from the basement and the existing furniture in the parlor, creating a comfortable but snug seating area. Kirsten had chosen to sit in one of the large overstuffed chairs. She'd recently cropped her hair and was letting it go gray as she embraced her fifties. Wife Linda was, as always, simultaneously regal and no-nonsense. Tall, substantial in a way that had intimidated criminal types when she'd been with the New Hope Police Force, Linda was aging beautifully. Kyle had once referred to her as Amazonian, a description she'd appreciated but asked him not to repeat.

Patty had taken on the task of making several trays of cheese, crackers, and crudités for the attendees. Two boxes of white wine had been set next to them with plastic wine glasses for those who wanted it. A large, elaborate plate of cookies was waiting in the kitchen to be enjoyed after the reading.

Danny was unphased by it all. He'd managed a restaurant for so many years that he was used to much bigger and more demanding crowds. He'd spent the past half hour making the rounds, introducing himself to people he didn't know and chatting briefly with those he did. Linda stood under the arch that separated the parlor from the dining room, sipping a glass of wine as she glanced approvingly around the room. Everyone looked to be having a good time except Kyle.

"Where are our houseguests?" Kyle asked Patty. She'd been quietly circulating among the crowd, picking up any used napkins and paper plates.

"They're here," she replied. "I saw them come in earlier. Most of them."

"Most of them?"

"Mr. Summit and Mr. Garland have not returned from wherever they went, but the others are here."

Kyle looked around. He spotted the two couples staying at the house. They gotten to know each other casually and had formed a four-person clique by the fireplace. He checked his watch: 6:45 p.m. The reading was set to start in fifteen minutes. He glanced at the stairs, hoping the remaining houseguests would come down soon. He didn't want any interruptions once Kirsten began reading from her book.

It's not your problem, he told himself. *This is Kirsten's event, you don't need to spend the night worrying how well it's going. Just relax, for godsake.*

But he knew it was useless. He would not relax until the event had gone successfully and everyone had left. Until then, he would keep looking at his watch every two minutes, worried something would go wrong.

Scott was furious. He'd been waiting two hours for Harold to return his call. He'd spent most of that time pacing the suite — lying in bed for ten minutes, then walking back and forth to the window before lying down again and staring at his phone as if he could will it to ring. He was still humiliated from his experience at the reception. Were all writers this awful? Is that why Harold had refused to invite him to conferences before, to protect him from this kind of rudeness? Or had they been right, and Harold's success was based on a lie and a theft? Only Harold could answer those questions, and he had disappeared.

Scott looked at the bedside clock. The reading was in ten minutes. He could hear people downstairs talking and laughing. Was Harold down there already? Had his phone battery died and he'd simply been unable to call Scott back? *Of course* he had left the reception, given the shabby treatment to which he'd been subjected. Knowing Harold, he'd probably gone for another long walk to clear his head and let go of the righteous indignation he surely felt. To be accused of something as heinous as plagiarism, the highest of crimes in the literary world, was to be challenged to a duel to the death. It was the kind of thing that could end a career, even one as established and lucrative as Harold's.

Scott jumped out of bed, certain now that Harold was downstairs mingling with the others, having a drink or three to flush out his well-deserved anger. He checked himself in the mirror, made sure his shirt was tucked into his slacks, and hurried out of the room.

Gladys was not feeling victorious. Her great scene, the one she'd rehearsed and played out in her mind for weeks, had had the effect she'd wanted on everyone but her. Summit was finished, she was sure of it. Even if he still churned out his hackneyed thrillers based on a character she'd created, his standing in the literary world would be so diminished he would not be invited to anything more impressive than an exterminators convention. She should have been rejoicing; instead, she was glum and agitated.

"Sweetheart, let's go downstairs," Carol said. "We promised we'd be there."

"I've never read her books, this Kirsten whoever."

"It doesn't matter. She's doing a reading and we said we would attend. Besides, she's got a wife with quite a colorful background."

Gladys forgot her malaise for a moment. "Really? How did I not know this?"

"You've been preoccupied, it's understandable. But I've done my homework: not only has the wife, Linda Sikorsky, helped to apprehend several murderers, she did it with Kyle Callahan."

Gladys looked at her, surprised. "The owner of this place?"

"One and the same. It may be among the reasons they left New York. We could ask him, in a nice way."

"I'm not asking him anything," said Gladys, but she was now quickly getting ready to go downstairs. There wasn't much preparation needed; she had no intention of changing her clothes just to sit in a chair listening to a writer she'd never heard of read from a book she would never buy. "The wife sounds interesting. I suppose that's worth an hour of our time."

As was her habit, Gladys slipped her feet into her Skechers and left the room, not waiting for Carol to leave with her.

Carol hurried behind, and a moment later they were descending the stairs to the sound of chairs being adjusted as the crowd took their seats and the reading began.

CHAPTER 26

Kirsten McLellan was delighted to be sitting in a room reading selected portions of her third book. Selling her real estate business and becoming a writer was not something she'd ever imagined doing. But here she was, reading another section from *Murder at the the Crossroads: A A Rox Harmony Mystery*, while two dozen people sat listening around her.

Kyle watched the audience. He'd read all three books in the series, easily identifying Linda's personality and habits in the main character. He was less familiar with Philadelphia, where the series was set, but he'd been there several times and was impressed with Kirsten's details of the city.

He looked around the room again, scanning the faces. He knew many of the people by sight, either as neighbors he'd spoken to, or as local residents he'd seen around town. The houseguests were there, as they'd promised to be, with the exceptions of Joseph Garland and Harold Summit. Kyle thought Garland might be in his room—he hadn't seem him come back that day, but the man moved like a shadow and could easily have come in without being seen. Harold Summit was another story. Kyle could see worry on Scott's face as he kept glancing from Kirsten to the front door, anxiously waiting for his husband to get there.

"I have one more excerpt," Kirsten said, as she flipped to the back of the book. "I don't want to spoil anything ..."

"We've got books you can buy for that!" Linda said, causing Kirsten to blush.

Kirsten continued: "It's from chapter sixteen, after Rox finds a note someone slipped in her car door. She's sure it's the killer again, taunting her."

Kirsten was about to start reading highlighted paragraphs when the front door opened.

Sergeant Bryan Hoyt stopped in the doorway, surprised to see a crowd in the parlor.

Kyle recognized him immediately. Sergeant Hoyt, like the rest of the Lambertville Police Department, was a familiar sight around town. Kyle had interacted with him several times on the street.

Hoyt was a handsome thirty-something, on the shorter side of six feet, with close-cropped brown hair showing signs of premature graying. He was wearing casual clothes, and Kyle thought at first he'd come late for the reading. Hoyt soon dispelled that misconception when he closed the door and walked into the room, stopping Kirsten from proceeding.

"I'm sorry to interrupt," Hoyt said. "I'm Sergeant Bryan Hoyt of the Lambertville Police." The introduction was unnecessary for many of the people there. "There's been an incident with one of the guests staying here."

A woman Kyle knew only as Rita turned to her companion and said, "This is part of it, the whole mystery thing. We'll probably have to solve the murder now. You know, they give us clues and we figure out who did it, like one of those escape rooms."

Moving closer to the circle, Hoyt said, "This is not pretend, unfortunately."

Scott slumped in his seat. He'd gone pale. "It's Harold, isn't it?"

"And you are?" asked Hoyt.

Standing from his chair, Scott said, "I'm Scott Harris, his husband. Was he arrested for something?"

"No, Sir, he wasn't," Hoyt replied. "May we speak somewhere privately?"

That was the moment Kyle knew Harold Summit was dead.

CHAPTER 27

The reading had continued awkwardly. Kirsten cut it short, flipping to a final section she had dogeared in her book, and rushing through a last few paragraphs. Only a handful of attendees stayed around to buy books and have them signed. A few others helped themselves to cookies and a gulp or two of wine before hurrying out of the house.

Among the ones who stayed was Bryan Hoyt. He'd had a conversation with Scott in the kitchen that lasted until Kirsten was finished reading. Scott had quietly slipped past the others and gone upstairs, visibly shaken. Then, when everyone got up and either left or headed into the dining room to have a book autographed, Hoyt positioned himself discreetly by the fireplace.

Kyle glanced across the room at Danny, nodding for him to take charge of the event while he spoke to Hoyt.

"I'd ask you if something was wrong," Kyle said to the sergeant, "but that's obvious. Is Mr. Summit in some kind of trouble?"

Hoyt extended his hand, shaking Kyle's. "I think we're about to have the longest conversation we've had since you moved to town, Mr. Callahan."

"Please, call me Kyle. I know something about you ..."

"And I know a few things about you."

Kyle's brow shot up. Had the detective been digging into his background? Why would he do that, and what had he found?

"I'm not sure how to take that," Kyle said.

"You've had an interesting life," Hoyt replied, with no trace of malice.

"If you're talking about my past experiences with murderers ..."

Hoyt shrugged: what else would he be talking about?

"I've left that behind me," Kyle continued. "Danny and I moved to Lambertville to start a new phase in life. We're here because it's peaceful. We can run a bed and breakfast, keep a low profile."

"This is a small city. Nobody keeps a low profile."

"So I'm discovering."

Hoyt looked past Kyle into the dining room. "I'll need to talk to the houseguests. Not the visitors who came for the reading, just the ones who checked in. And you and Mr. Durban, of course, and the staff. I understand you have two employees living here."

Kyle felt a knot tighten in his gut. "You still haven't said what this is about."

"Harold Summit was found dead in the Raritan canal, not far from Lambertville Station."

"Maybe he drowned?" Kyle said, posing it as a question. The canal was not a place anyone swam; it was more of a long, wide ditch with water.

"That's possible," Hoyt replied, "but someone put a bullet in him first. Now, about the staff and houseguests."

"Yes, of course. Shall I bring you a list in the morning?"

Hoyt frowned. "The morning is too late. I'll wait here."

The next half hour felt to Kyle like the longest he'd lived through for some time. He'd nodded after Hoyt's last words, then gone into the dining room to watch what was now a marred, nearly failed book signing come to a close. Finally, when everyone had left, he told Patty and Justin to stay around, and he told Danny it was going to be a long night.

CHAPTER 28

Please don't leave town.

Scott kept thinking about the last thing Hoyt said to him when their conversation in the kitchen ended. Harold was dead and somebody had made him that way. Interrogations would ensue, questions would be asked and re-asked, possibly until someone broke down and confessed. *Isn't that how it works?* Scott wondered. *They sit you in a room and harass you into admitting your guilt.* He'd seen enough shows on the ID Channel to have a good idea of where this was all headed, and it made him sick.

There was the matter, too, of Harold's death. When Hoyt first announced himself to the room, Scott assumed Harold had been busted with his precious little silver case. He'd told Harold many times not to take it out with him. Something as simple as a traffic stop could lead to the discovery of his travelling stash. And then, when Hoyt told him bluntly that Harold had been found in the canal, he'd assumed Harold's heart had given way under the daily pressure of a cocaine habit. When Hoyt finally said Harold had been shot, Scott was horrified ... and very nervous. He'd been too quick to tell Hoyt he was at the house all day; he'd had to amend his whereabouts, admitting he'd met Harold for lunch and gone to the reception that afternoon, where Harold had not shown up. *Oh my God,* he'd thought, tuning out whatever Hoyt was saying, *Harold was probably floating in the canal while I was being mistreated by those awful people with their cheap cocktails.*

The kitchen was not the proper place for questioning. There were two dozen people in the parlor. Scott had just been told his husband was murdered. And there was nowhere to sit in the kitchen. Hoyt had kept things as simple and brief as possible. He'd told Scott the basics facts—Harold's body had been spotted by a man riding his bicycle along the path next to the canal; the police had been called, and Harold had been retrieved from the water with a bullet in him. Hoyt did not say where the bullet had entered Harold, or speculate on who may have fired it: was it the result of a random act, or had Harold been targeted for one reason or another? Hoyt said nothing about these things, and when he was finished he told Scott to stay in town; there would be proper interviews at the police station the next day. Worried about his own position, Scott had provided as much of an alibi as he could. He had witnesses, he was sure of it — the house staff, the cruel writers toasting their own importance while they accused Harold of plagiarism. He could retrace his steps in detail, and he'd been seen everywhere along the way.

His grief over Harold's death had quickly been tempered by the realization he would soon be a rich man. Harold had no children, and the prenup Scott signed came into effect only if they divorced. Harold's fortune, while modest, was enough for Scott to live comfortably the rest of his life.

He'd gone directly to their room after his conversation with the sergeant. He could feel the people at the reading staring at him as he hurried upstairs. He didn't care. Everyone would soon know what they'd spoken about.

Sitting on the edge of the bed, he began thinking of alibi witnesses and appropriate reactions to the fact he was now a widower. He got up and went to the dresser, looking in the large mirror above it. *What did grief look like?* he wondered. *Was a frown sufficient? And how do actors make themselves cry?* It was a skill he would have to learn before morning.

CHAPTER 29

By eleven o'clock that night Sergeant Hoyt had interviewed everyone but Kyle, Danny, and Joseph Garland. He'd questioned them in the parlor while Patty cleared the dining room and fidgeted in the kitchen, anxious to finish her job. Kyle knew she would not go to bed until the rooms had been cleaned and restored to their normal condition. Justin, on the other hand, had gone upstairs seeming nervous and in a hurry to get away from it all.

The other guests had not taken long to answer Hoyt's questions. Whatever information they'd given Hoyt had been quick and perfunctory. Kyle guessed it was because they had little to offer except their whereabouts the past several hours.

Finally, it was Kyle and Danny's turn to answer questions. Hoyt did not object to them sitting together on the couch while he took an armchair he'd pulled close, talking to them across the coffee table. He used both a small handheld recorder he set on the table and a pocket notepad with a pen.

"Do you think anyone in this house was involved in Mr. Summit's murder?" Kyle asked.

"That's why I'm speaking to everyone," Hoyt replied. "And I'd appreciate it if you left the questioning to me."

Kyle couldn't help it: he felt that old adrenaline rush that came with picking up the scent of a criminal. He thought he'd left it behind him, but it was like the smell of wine after not drinking for three years, or the taste of something spicy after a long bland diet. He knew Danny could sense it in him from the way he watched Kyle speaking, wary of his husband's intentions.

"When did Summit and his partner check in?" Hoyt asked.

"Yesterday morning," Kyle said. "They were early. The Millimans and the Kopeck-Stillers were already here—they'd arrived on Saturday. Joseph Garland came Sunday afternoon. Summit and Harris on Wednesday, followed shortly by Gladys Finch and her wife, Carol."

"Is that a full house?"

"Completely," said Danny. It was the first thing he'd said

since they had sat down. "What is it you're trying to find out, Sergeant?"

"The facts," replied Hoyt. "And anything that comes out of them. Where's Joseph Garland, by the way?"

Kyle and Danny looked at each other and shrugged.

"We don't know," Kyle said. "He's an odd man. He told us he's here researching his family history. It's very trendy now, everyone wants to know where they came from. Garland likes his privacy, and he comes and goes as he pleases. He hasn't really mixed with anyone."

"And do you know why the others are here? Their reasons for coming to Lambertville?"

"Yes, for the most part," said Kyle. "The Millimans were in town for a wedding, and the Kopeck-Stillers are on vacation. Summit and Finch are here for the authors conference."

Hoyt made several quick notes on his pad.

"When was the last time you saw Summit leave the house?"

"This morning, actually," Kyle said. "He left for the conference after breakfast. He didn't come back. Scott Harris went to meet him for lunch—he mentioned that's where he was going—and after that I didn't pay any attention. We had the reading to prepare for."

"Was your staff here?"

"Our staff?" asked Kyle, as if he hadn't understood the question.

"Patty Langley and Justin Stritch. They live here, I believe."

"You believe correctly," Danny said.

"You can't think either of them was involved?" said Kyle.

"At the moment I don't think anything. That's why I'm questioning everyone."

"Yes, of course," said Kyle. "They both live here on the third floor. Justin ran some errands this morning, and he picked up extra chairs at the church this afternoon. Patty was here all day, as far as I know."

"As far as you know?"

Kyle thought about it. "She spends a lot of time in her room when she's not working, which isn't often. The woman's obsessed with cleaning."

Hoyt stared at Kyle, watching his face. "And where were you this afternoon?"

Kyle was shocked. Was Hoyt really suggesting he may have had something to do with Summit's murder?

"I was here most of the day, preparing."

"Most of the day?"

"Well, yes. I went for a walk in town ..." His expression changed as he remembered seeing Harold Summit veer onto the path. "I saw him, briefly. He was walking ahead of me and I thought about catching up to him, then he turned onto the trail. What time did you say he was killed?"

"I didn't," said Hoyt.

"Right, you didn't. But that was this morning. Maybe I was the last person to see him alive. Oh my God ..."

"The last person to see him alive was the one who killed him," Hoyt said.

He closed his notebook and slipped it into his jacket pocket. He reached out and took the recorder from the coffee table, turning it off.

"I'll have more questions tomorrow, especially about your encounter in town."

"It wasn't an encounter," Kyle protested. "I told you, I left him alone, and then I went to the Brightside Diner."

"Let me guess," Hoyt said. "You have a receipt."

Kyle didn't like the implications of that. "I do," he said.

"We keep meticulous records," Danny added. "I was in the restaurant business for thirty years, it's a habit."

"And a convenient one," said Hoyt, as he stood up to leave.

"What's that supposed to mean?" Danny asked defensively.

Hoyt shrugged: maybe it meant something, maybe it meant nothing.

"Do you have enough to go on?" Kyle asked, disappointed that Hoyt had not asked for his input. He'd already begun imagining motives and lines of inquiry. Should he tell Hoyt about the hostility between Finch and Summit? What about the time lapse Patty had brought to his attention, when Justin was gone longer than he'd needed to be? And would all of it sound like misdirection, as if he were trying to steer Hoyt away from himself?

Hoyt ignored the question. He pushed his chair back to its spot.

"I don't need to tell you not to leave town. I've already told the others."

"The couples?" Kyle said as he stood up from the couch. "But they're checking out Monday."

"Not the couples, although that's really none your business at the moment. The others. The women, Finch and Dupree, were at the conference and may know more than they think they do. The staff lives here, so they'll be around anyway. And I'll find Garland one way or the other. When you see him, please tell him to contact me."

Hoyt took a business card out of his wallet and handed it to Danny, who was standing now.

As if he could read Kyle's mind, Hoyt said, "This is a murder investigation, gentlemen. Interference is not welcome."

"Of course not," Danny said.

"Absolutely not!" Kyle echoed. But he knew better. It was like telling a child he could have nothing in a candy store after dragging him inside.

Kyle and Danny walked Hoyt to the door.

"You'll be hearing from me," Hoyt said as he shook each man's hand and walked down the front steps.

Danny closed the door. Turning to Kyle, he said, "Don't."

"Don't what?"

"You know what I mean."

"I won't get involved." The promise sounded halfhearted even to Kyle. "But I can't help thinking about it."

And that is precisely what he did.

CHAPTER 30

Kyle woke up agitated. He had to pursue the truth of what happened to Harold Summit as surely as he had to breathe and eat. And besides, the victim was a registered guest at their place of business. If someone there was involved in Summit's murder, Kyle needed to know. The reputation and survival of Passion House could be at stake.

Danny slept later than Kyle and had not had his sleep disturbed by thoughts of murder.

"Good morning," Kyle said, patting Danny lightly on the arm before slipping out of bed. He quickly showered and dressed, and was eating a bagel at the kitchen table when he heard Danny start his morning routine. The cats had taken their places at his feet, expecting him to share whatever he had on his plate.

"Who do you think killed him?" he asked Wilma, as he dipped his finger in cream cheese on his plate and let her lick it off. "Gladys Finch had some resentment toward Mr. Summit, that was obvious. But was it enough to commit murder? And frankly, I don't see her as the killer type. She's not aging well—she can barely make it up the stairs. On the other hand, he was shot, and anyone can pull a trigger."

Leonard was not happy that Kyle had given a treat to Wilma first. He pushed her out of the way with his head, demanding an equal portion. Kyle offered him the same fingertip covered in cream cheese and he licked it up.

"There's Scott Harris, of course," Kyle said, thinking out loud. "They always look at the spouse first. Summit was a wealthy man ... unless he wasn't, and he was putting on an appearance. Do you suppose there was an insurance policy? Or maybe he met someone in town. Maybe it was just robbery, but in Lambertville? On a public trail? That's the last option, don't you think? Nothing about this says random."

"Who are you talking to?"

Kyle jerked around in his chair. Danny was standing in his favorite white plush robe in the doorway.

"Myself," said Kyle, his face flushed.

"I hope so. Cats can't talk back. By the way, my money's on the husband."

Before Kyle could say anything, Danny turned and headed down the hallway. A moment later Kyle heard the bathroom door close.

"Let's leave Danny out of this, shall we?" Kyle said to the cats. "I think he'd prefer that anyway. I'm going over to the house and see what kind of wreckage there is."

The parlor and dining room were quiet. Mornings were always slow to start, with guests trickling downstairs or scattered around making use of the free WiFi.

Patty was still setting the table when Kyle walked in. To his surprise, no one had yet come downstairs, including Justin.

"Where's your help?" Kyle asked. "He's usually here by now."

"Justin isn't feeling well," Patty said, placing paper napkins to the left of each plate. "He conveys his apologies and expects to be down later."

"He's going to the police station to make a statement, I presume," said Kyle.

"I assume so," said Patty. "We've all been asked to."

Kyle waited for more; Patty said nothing, moving on to the silverware. He looked at the stairs. "Where is everyone?"

"After last night, I'd guess they're not in the most convivial mood."

Kyle knew she was right. He was surprised anyone would come to breakfast after what happened. "Maybe we should have canceled it."

"It's part of the package," she reminded him. "They don't have to eat, but it must be provided."

"Of course."

The somber atmosphere was interrupted when several guests began making their way into the dining room. Gladys and Carol could be heard walking to the staircase, and just behind them, Scott Harris.

A few minutes later Danny arrived and everyone was seated at the table, minus Justin and Joseph Garland. Pleasantries were exchanged without enthusiasm, as the weight of a murder clouded the room.

Kyle decided to check in on Garland before taking his seat. He excused himself and went to Garland's room. After waiting a moment, he knocked.

"Mr. Garland?" he said, leaning into the closed door. "Joseph?"

No answer came. He knocked again. After considering the consequences of going into a guest's room, he decided it was more important to make sure the old man was alright than to respect his seclusion.

Kyle gently opened the door, expecting to see Garland sitting at the small desk, or working on some ancestry chart on the bed. Instead, the bed was empty. The spread was undisturbed. Joseph Garland had not come back.

"That's odd," Kyle said to himself. "Where did you go?"

He closed the door and hurried back to the dining room, joining the others for what became the most morose meal he'd ever shared.

Justin never came down for breakfast. Kyle saw him only in passing after the table had been cleared and everyone had gone back to their rooms. Today was apparently not one for adventure or sightseeing, and Kyle hoped no one had decided to leave early. He couldn't very well keep their money under the circumstances.

"I'm going to the police station," Justin said, taking an apple from the fruit bowl in the parlor.

"Don't you want some breakfast?" Kyle asked.

Danny had gone back to the guest house, leaving Kyle and Patty to clean up.

Holding up the apple, Justin said, "I'm not very hungry."

"I imagine not," said Kyle. "Nobody was."

Most of the breakfast had gone uneaten. A police investigation can do that to the appetite.

"What are you going to tell Sergeant Hoyt?" Kyle asked.

Patty was lingering in the kitchen doorway, making sure she heard any conversation.

Justin sighed and said, "The truth. Then I'll tell you and Mr. Durban, and you can decide if you still want me here."

Well, well, thought Kyle. It appeared Justin had broken the rules after all, and with a murder victim.

"Did you have sex?" Kyle asked bluntly.

Avoiding Kyle's gaze, Justin replied, "No, but we were going to. Obviously that won't happen now."

"Obviously," said Patty.

Kyle had forgotten she was there. He glared at her and she disappeared into the kitchen.

"We'll talk when you get back," Kyle said.

Justin hurried out of the house, leaving Kyle with the added burden of deciding the young man's future. He had one dead houseguest and another one missing. He had potential suspects staying in the rooms. He had the future of Passion House hanging in the balance. It was all too much, too heavy for him, a weight he knew he couldn't carry alone.

It was time to make a phone call.

PART II

A Friend in Need

CHAPTER 31

Linda wasn't terribly surprised to see Kyle in her kitchen asking for help. Murder had brought them together eight years earlier, and in her more reflective moments she knew it would always be part of their bond. She'd been a homicide detective then, having worked her way up in the New Hope Police Department over the course of a twenty-year career. He'd been a witness of sorts, friends with a victim whose death had quickly gone from possible accident to definite homicide. Kyle and Danny had been at Pride Lodge for one of their weekend getaways from the stresses of Manhattan. The dead man, Teddy Pembroke, had worked at the lodge and was a familiar presence around the grounds until they found him dead at the bottom of an empty swimming pool. Detective Linda Sikorsky questioned the men along with all of the guests and staff, and when it was over, when one killer had been caught while another slipped away into the night, she and the couple from New York City became friends. For several years that friendship included crossing paths with, and chasing down, a few very bad people. One of them, Diedrich Keller, almost ended both their lives. That had shaken them deeply and sent Kyle onto a therapist's couch. By then Linda had retired, settling into her house in the woods with her new wife. A few years later Kyle and Danny made the move to Lambertville, and here he was, bringing another murder to her doorstep like a cat who's caught a bird in its mouth. She had confided in Kirsten that while she was delighted to have them live nearby, something told her the darkness they'd known would find them again. *Welcome, old friend Death, we've been expecting you.*

The house was on a road with few neighbors, each home separated by land and woods. Linda had inherited it from her aunt, whom she'd visited many times over the years. Celeste Meadows had always been among Linda's champions. She had also been the first person Linda told she was gay. Celeste had thought nothing of it, as if her favorite niece had informed her she was thinking of majoring in biology. "That's nice," Celeste had said, before moving on to the pressing topic of deer overpopulation.

It was a small house that had taken some getting used to, especially for Kirsten. Linda knew writing novels had helped her wife not regret moving from New Hope to rural New Jersey. They were only fifteen minutes apart, but as different as could be. One was a bustling town, the other a patch of land surrounded by wildlife. Everything had turned out well: Linda had her vintage-everything store to run in New Hope, Kirsten had her novels to write, and they had each other. The last thing she needed was Kyle showing up with another murder to solve.

"I don't have any idea who killed Harold Summit," Kyle said. He was sitting at Linda's small kitchen table. A window above the sink looked out on an aging driveway, with trees just beyond.

"How could you?" asked Linda. She'd made coffee for them both. She was grateful Kirsten had gone to Stockton for a few supplies at the general store. It gave her time to talk to Kyle alone.

"I'm glad he wasn't murdered at the house," Kyle continued. "Imagine what that would do for business." He blushed, ashamed at what he'd said. "I don't mean it the way it sounds. It's awful that he's dead. But I'm concerned whoever killed him is staying with us."

"Another houseguest."

"Yes."

"Why would any of them want to kill him? That's a little high profile."

Linda had read one of Summit's novels and not cared for it, but she knew he was a popular author on the B-list.

"Resentment does strange things to people," Kyle said. "I got the feeling one of the other guests, Gladys Finch, had some issues with him. And Justin ..."

Linda knew they'd had concerns about their young staff member. "What about Justin?"

"He either did something with Summit, some sex thing, or was about to. He admitted it. We'll probably have to let him go."

"If he's not the killer."

Kyle looked at her. "We'll definitely have to let him go if he's the killer."

It was a moment of levity in a serious conversation.

"What do you want from me, Kyle?" Linda asked, although she knew the answer.

"I want to look into it."

"Look into what?"

"Harold Summit's murder."

There, he'd said it, stating the obvious.

"Sergeant Bryan Hoyt, from the Lambertville police ..."

"I know Bryan," Linda said.

"He's questioning everyone again today, or at least the people he needs to. I don't want to interfere —"

Linda laughed, unable to stop herself. "Of course you want to interfere! That's why you're here." Sipping her coffee while she thought it over, she said, "I have to tell Kirsten, of course."

Kyle knew he'd hooked her. Linda was a detective by nature. It's what she'd always wanted to do as a cop, the path she'd pursued and achieved. He wondered if she, too, had missed the hunt. Seeing the gleam in her eyes, he knew she had.

"Tell me what you know," Linda said, sitting at attention.

Kyle began giving her all the details he could, some clear, most sketchy.

The excitement of the chase had begun.

CHAPTER 32

Sitting on the edge of the bed, Gladys felt something she rarely experienced, something foreign and unsettling: she felt *guilty*. She'd banished things like guilt and regret to the outer reaches of her soul when she'd been a mere tomboy bearing up under the criticism of a mother who had wanted her to look frilly, to *feel* frilly. Gladys had resisted then and never stopped. Telling Gladys Finch what to do or say, who not to offend, was as futile as telling the wind not to blow. But here she was, thinking about the murder of Harold Summit and somehow, for some reason, feeling responsible.

"It's like when someone you love dies and you never got to tell them how much they meant to you," Gladys said, staring at her sneakers.

"You hated him," Carol reminded her. "You exposed him as a plagiarist."

"Yes I did, and now he's dead."

"You had nothing to do with it!"

"But still ... he died with my very public accusation ringing in his ears."

Carol went to the bed and sat next to her. She put a hand on Gladys's leg, rubbing gently. "He wasn't there, sweetheart. He didn't hear you."

"But they told him what I said and he ran off, and someone killed him." Gladys sighed deeply. "Perhaps that was a kindness. Suppose he couldn't live with the shame? It may be better to have someone take your life than to take your own in disgrace."

"I doubt Harold Summit would have killed himself over this. More likely he'd deny it and just write another book. Money has a way of soothing any shame one feels in making it."

"I wouldn't know," Gladys said, surprised by Carol's insight. "I've never made any."

Gladys stared out the window, wishing they hadn't come here. She didn't really feel all that badly about the death of Harold Summit, a man who had deprived her of fame and fortune that should have been hers.

But did he rob you of these things, Gladys? she wondered. *Would you have written more than a short story about Connie Dark, a brief experiment in a genre you don't even read? Or was this all your bruised and fragile ego? Was this the tomboy Gladys telling her mother to leave her alone, she'd wear coveralls and play in the mud if she damned well pleased? You're not a nice person, Gladys. Maybe that's just who you are.*

"Maybe that's just who I am," Gladys murmured.

"What, dear?" asked Carol.

Gladys turned and smiled at her. "Nothing, Carol. Nothing at all."

Justin felt trapped waiting in the front seating area of the Lambertville Police Station. He'd spent the night sleeping fitfully between dreams of dead men in canals, and long periods staring at the ceiling while he planned his escape. But to where? And why? He knew he had nothing to do with the old man's murder. He also knew he would be an easy target, a convenient fall guy, if the police chose to pin it on him and call it case closed. He'd watched enough TV shows to know this happened: someone with a questionable past had contact with the victim in the victim's last hours, and that someone became the focus of their investigation. It wasn't unheard of for an innocent man to spend years in prison, only to be exonerated with some new development in DNA analysis. Would it be him? He'd broken a few hearts. He'd even stolen on occasion, but only things he thought wouldn't be missed. On the other hand, he'd cleaned up his act and had been on the straight and narrow for a few years now. The only way the police would know about his past is if they asked too many questions of too many people.

That's what they do, Justin, he thought.. *They ask questions. Especially that sergeant. He's kind of hot. Maybe if I flirt with him ...* The thought made him laugh, a moment of gallows humor at a dark time. *Yeah, sure, flirt with him all the way to trial. Insist you're innocent while they expose your life for everyone to see — the drugs, the men, the petty crime. Go ahead, Justin, flirt with the man and say goodbye to your freedom.*

He glanced up and saw the young woman who staffed the front desk staring at him.

"Are you okay?" she asked.

"I'm fine," Justin said.

"Sergeant Hoyt will be right with you."

"Thanks."

He wondered if it was too late to run. He could excuse himself, say he'd left something in the car, although he'd walked to the station and didn't have a car. She wouldn't know. He could head up the street and just keep going. He had his wallet and the clothes on his back. What more did he need, really?

"Mr. Stritch ..."

Justin looked up. Bryan Hoyt was standing in front of him, extending his hand. Justin got up, shook Hoyt's hand and immediately wondered if Hoyt noticed how damp his palm was.

"Sergeant, nice to see you again."

What a stupid, ridiculous thing to say, he thought. Seeing Hoyt again was dreadful. A man was dead and he, Justin Stritch, may be high on a short list of suspects. He had to tell the truth. The truth was easy to remember, the truth was what really happened.

"Right this way," Hoyt said.

Justin followed him past the desk and down a hallway. He wondered if that's how it felt to walk into prison. He listened a moment for the sound of steel bars closing behind him, swearing he could almost hear them.

Scott had never regretted anything as much as he regretted coming back to Lambertville. It hadn't even been his idea. Harold had been feeling stuck for the past year, talking about the next chapter in a new Connor Dark novel Scott knew he wasn't writing. He was well aware that Harold spent his computer time obsessively reading news articles and viewing pornography, then insisting he'd been working on an outline or creating characters. It was a sham even Harold knew he couldn't sustain. Then the announcement for the Mystery Authors Alliance conference showed up in Harold's email, and suddenly that was going to remedy his creative malaise. Harold could come to Lambertville and be somebody again. He could mingle with writers he wouldn't otherwise give the time of day, sign dozens of books and maybe get a speaking gig or two. Then he and Scott could return to Los Angeles, and a reinvigorated Harold could get back to the business of writing. Instead, he ended up dead in a shabby canal near a few graffiti-covered railcars.

"And I'm the first person they'll look at," Scott said to himself.

He was sitting in one of the suite's armchairs, where he'd been since shortly before dawn. Sleep had threatened him a few times over the course of the night, but had been chased away by worry and fear. The one thing missing from his emotional response was any deep grief over the death of his husband. He knew he should be devastated, and more importantly, he should *appear* devastated. But it had also made him wealthy, or at least comfortable, something easily seen as motive.

He had no idea where to begin. He'd endured breakfast with the others, thankful none of them had asked him about the previous night's events. What do you say to someone whose spouse was found dead, and who'd been informed of it in the kitchen of a bed and breakfast? He knew they were curious, and why wouldn't they be? But it was like having some terrible disease or a terminal condition—everyone knows, but nobody wants to talk about it.

Then he'd retired to his room and watched the news again. It hadn't taken long for word to get out. He assumed someone had tweeted about it or shared their alarm on a Facebook page. By the time he'd gotten out of bed that morning, the world knew Harold Summit was dead and foul play was suspected. It was also a demonstration of the limits of Harold's fame. He was no Stephen King. His novels were popular, but there would not be a throng of media descending on Passion House to interview the guests and staff. Harold had been a big-ish fish in a medium-sized pond. And, frankly, Connor Dark had been getting long in the tooth. Tastes had changed, Harold's fan base had aged and shrunk. It was a celebrity death, certainly, but not the major one Harold had hoped for when his time came. And in none of the accounts was there mention of Scott Harris, the grieving husband. Harold had hidden him in his professional life, and in death that's all that counted. Why would any reporter ask how he was holding up when so few of them knew he existed?

Maybe that's why you're not so crushed by this, Scott thought, as he reached for the remote and turned the television off. That and the bank account, and the life insurance policy, and the house in

Glendale, and the royalties. He stared out the window, wondering if he could hire a ghost writer to finish whatever Harold had written of the next Connor Dark thriller. Or maybe he could do it himself. He'd always wanted to be a writer ... or a singer, or an actor, or just famous.

He had options now.

CHAPTER 33

Linda followed Kyle back from Kingwood in her car, and he imagined her thinking things through on the drive. She was like that: deliberative, cautious, concerned much more with evidence than with speculation. It had been a long time since their last teaming, when she'd helped him with a cold case that had brought them into deadly contact with a mafia queen and destroyed a powerful New York City District Attorney. Neither of them had expected to find themselves searching for a killer again.

Patty knew Linda from her visits to the house and greeted her warmly when they came in.

"Are you okay, Miss Sikorsky?" Patty asked, touching Linda's arm in a gesture as close to a hug as Patty ever offered.

"I'm fine, Patty," Linda replied. "Kirsten and I aren't the ones dealing with what happened. Save your concern for Kyle and Danny, and certainly for Mr. Summit's husband."

"The death is a shock," Patty said. "May I get you something? Coffee or tea?"

"We're fine," Kyle interrupted. "Linda has agreed to help me ... *consider* things. To puzzle it out, so to speak, in case there's something we've missed that could help Sergeant Hoyt."

"Of course. I'll get out of your way."

Patty touched Linda's arm again, then headed upstairs to her room.

They'd gone over what little Kyle knew at Linda's house. He'd told her about answering Hoyt's questions at the end of the evening, and about Justin's confession and the uncomfortable position it put them in.

"I don't see how we can let him work here," Kyle said.

"I think you have bigger things to worry about right now," Linda replied. "You've had a houseguest murdered. That's not something you can keep secret."

"No, we can't. We've already had calls from a few reporters. I don't know how they found out where he was staying. We're not commenting for now. I expect a TV van at some point."

"They're probably at the canal getting footage from where he

111

died."

Linda took another look around the parlor. "We were talking about Garland earlier."

"Right," said Kyle. "He's an odd man. Not creepy, necessarily, and he seems harmless, just odd."

"Because he doesn't talk about himself?"

Kyle felt a twinge of shame for judging the old man. He didn't take photos or selfies, or even have a smartphone — Kyle had seen him using a flip phone once or twice. Aside from that, he hadn't displayed any electronics at all.

"We should take a look in his room," Kyle said.

"I thought you weren't going to do that," Linda replied, reminding Kyle of something he'd told her at the house.

"The more I think about it, the more it seems acceptable. He is staying here, and we have a right as the owners of Passion House to inspect our own property. Plus, he hasn't been seen since yesterday afternoon. He may need help."

"You're sure he didn't come back?"

"Patty said she never saw him return, and she sees everything."

Kyle led her to Garland's room.

"On the other hand," he said outside Garland's door, "she does sleep occasionally, and he could have slipped in without anyone seeing him."

"That makes him sound suspicious. Maybe he isn't hiding anything at all. Maybe he just doesn't think his life is anyone's business."

"Or maybe he came back when Patty was asleep and he's been in his room all this time. He could have had a stroke or a heart attack and be on his bed right now. 'Exigent circumstances,' I think they call it."

Kyle leaned into the door, knocked and spoke softly but firmly.

"Mr. Garland? Hello? Joseph?"

Getting no response, he waited a moment and knocked again. He put his hand on the doorknob, called out one more time and opened the door.

The room's occupant had kept it as clean and neat as if he'd never been there. The bed was made exactly as Patty had left it the morning before, and looked as if Joseph Garland had not slept in it since he'd arrived. A small suitcase had been slipped beneath the bed; they could see it from the doorway when they entered. The nightstand had a worn Day Planner on it that looked as if Garland had been using it for a decade.

Kyle walked over to the closet. The door had been left ajar. He eased it open and saw what he'd suspected: Joseph Garland had two identical suits, except for color, to the one he was wearing the last time they saw him. That was all. There may be underwear and socks in a dresser drawer, but Kyle was not going to find out. So far he had not done anything to invade Garland's privacy, only to make sure he wasn't in the room needing emergency medical attention.

"I think we should go now," Kyle said.

"Yes, we should. At least we know he's not here."

"And that's all we know, isn't it? Now do you understand what I'm talking about? Two suits in the closet, a Day Planner on the stand, a suitcase tucked under the bed. What does that tell you?"

"It tells me he's fastidious," Linda replied. "And that he travels light. There's nothing criminal about that."

"No, but there is something strange."

Kyle was interrupted by Patty stepping into the room. If she thought anything of them being there, it was lost in her emotion.

"They've found him," Patty said, breathless.

"Who?" Kyle asked.

Patty looked at him as if the answer was obvious. "Mr. Garland!" she exclaimed.

"You mean they caught him?" said Kyle. "Trying to leave town?"

"No! They found his body."

Kyle felt the floor shift beneath him. He and Linda were standing in the room of a second dead man who'd been staying at Passion House.

"It's on the news," Patty explained. "Some boys fishing in the river found a body lodged along the bank, near Stockton."

Stockton was a small town between Lambertville and Kingwood Township. No more than two blocks long, with a liquor store, general store and farmers market, it had a bridge going over the Delaware River into Pennsylvania.

"Maybe he jumped," Kyle said, thinking out loud.

"Excuse me?" said Linda.

"I'm just thinking out loud. He could have jumped off the bridge."

"He would have floated far past Stockton if he did," Linda pointed out. "Besides, you're getting ahead of yourself. We haven't even seen the news."

"I thought you should know," Patty said, having composed herself as best she could.

Kyle had forgotten she was there. He realized he and Linda had gone into Garland's room after his death. Had they implicated themselves in any way? Kyle's fingerprints would be in the room, of course, he owned the house. But the intrusion, the *snooping*, might look bad if Hoyt found out about it.

Patty left them, hurrying down the hallway.

"We should turn on the TV and see what they're saying about Garland," Linda said.

"Yes, but not in here, obviously."

As they started to leave the room, Kyle made a quick decision: he walked over and took Joseph Garland's Day Planner off the nightstand.

"What are you doing?" Linda asked. "That could be evidence."

"I know that. It could also tell us what he was up to."

"You have to put it back, Kyle, and you have to stay out of this room."

"I will," Kyle said as they left, "I just want to glance through it. Garland had a friend in New Hope, he told us that—they had dinner the first night he was here. I'd also like some idea of where he was going since he came to town. I'll just scan a few pages, put it back on the nightstand, and no one will be the wiser."

He could tell she did not approve of his actions, but she wasn't going to stop him. Either Joseph Garland was innocent and it was all a tragic coincidence, or his death was somehow connected to Harold Summit's murder. The complications were adding up, and an answer might be found in the Day Planner.

"Make us some coffee, will you?" Kyle said. "I'm going to the guest house to use the scanner. I'll be back in ten minutes."

Linda went into the kitchen as Kyle hurried out of the house, holding Joseph Garland's Day Planner close to his chest.

CHAPTER 34

"You're tampering with evidence."

Danny watched as Kyle took the Day Planner, butterflied it and scanned copies of the last several pages, as well as a contact section with names and phone numbers. They were at a shared desk in a corner of the living room where they'd set up office for business and personal use.

"We don't know it's evidence."

"Then why are you copying it in such a hurry? You're expecting another visit from Sergeant Hoyt, that's why, and you want to get this bit of questionable activity out of the way before he shows up. Does Linda approve of this?"

Danny knew Linda had come back with Kyle; he'd seen her car parked on the street.

Kyle left the question unanswered. He didn't want to implicate Linda in anything he'd chosen to do.

Danny knew about Joseph Garland's death the same way Patty had found out. The morning news had included a report on a second body found in the area. It was a Philadelphia station with a local stringer named Martha Ruiz who covered stories outside the metropolitan area. It wasn't yet known that both men had been staying at Passion House, but it soon would be. Danny expected Ruiz to show up any minute, shoving a microphone in their faces and asking for comment.

"I just want to look into some things," Kyle said, by way of excusing his actions. "You can't invade the privacy of a dead man."

"Of course you can! What if there are things he wouldn't want you to know about him?"

"Well, that's pretty much everything, isn't it? Think about it, Danny. He reserved his room for a week and paid in advance. He didn't interact with the other houseguests. He came and went at odd hours, and he was found dead on a river bank. Can that possibly be more invasive than me wanting to know a little more about him? He stayed in our house, our business. We almost have a right to know what he was up to."

"I caught the 'almost,'" Danny said. "You know what you're doing is shady, and I don't want any part of it."

Kyle finished scanning what he thought would be enough pages to serve his purpose, then turned in his chair to face Danny. "You've never wanted any part of it."

"It almost got me killed, in case you don't remember."

Kyle would never forget Danny's being abducted and nearly murdered in Diedrich Keller's basement, or what he'd had to do to stop that madman.

"Those images will be with me forever," Kyle said. "I don't want you involved. I've got Linda. And we don't have much time. You and I are due to see Sergeant Hoyt this afternoon to give statements. I'd like to see if there's anything Linda and I can find out before then. You just stay here in the guest house, distract yourself, whatever helps you stay calm."

"I am calm."

Kyle stood up and gave Danny a kiss. "I know what calm is for you, and this is not it. You're a wreck, you just hide it well."

Danny neither confirmed nor denied his emotional state. He walked Kyle to the door and held it open for him.

"Remember," Danny said, "behind every murder victim is a murderer."

"I love you," said Kyle, heading across the lawn to the house. He knew the truth of what Danny had said, and he was determined not to let his curiosity get him too close to the edge — just a few facts, an insight or two into the events of the past day and a half. After that it would be up to the police to find a killer, and up to Kyle and Danny to make sure Passion House survived.

CHAPTER 35

Linda was still in the kitchen when Kyle returned. She'd made coffee and was almost finished with hers when he came through the back door, holding the Day Planner and several copied sheets.

"Let me put this back first," he said, hurrying past her. He dropped the photocopied pages on the counter next to the coffee machine.

He took the Planner into Garland's room and placed it back on the nightstand, worrying for a moment that he hadn't placed it exactly as he'd found it. *That's ridiculous,* he thought. *Nobody else was ever in this room. Who would notice anyway?*

Moments later he was back in the kitchen. Linda was standing over the counter looking at the sheets Kyle had duplicated.

"Let me grab my coffee, then we can see what there is to see."

He got a mug from the cupboard and pored himself a cup, adding a splash of creamer from a quart of Half and Half Linda had left by the sink.

"Okay," he said finally. "Let's have a look."

He and Linda took the sheets and read over them. There wasn't much there, mostly scribblings in an old man's hand. One note said, "River Valley Bank," and another said, "Dinner with Paul, 7:30."

"There's no River Valley Bank around here that I know of," Kyle muttered, glancing over the other few pages.

"It's gone," said Linda.

Kyle looked at her, surprised.

"There was a River Valley Bank," she explained. "My aunt banked there."

"Celeste?" asked Kyle, referring to the aunt who'd left Linda her house.

"She's the only aunt I had. She used to do business with them, but it was at least ten years ago. They got bought out by New Jersey Savings and Loan."

"I've never heard of them, either."

"All these smaller banks get eaten up by the big ones. I think they're Chase now, I'm not sure. But back then it was River Valley and they had branches in several of the towns around here. Celeste's was in Lambertville."

Kyle thought about it and saw no immediate connection. That was the problem with someone as mysterious as Joseph Garland: nothing would be obvious because they'd known so little about him.

"Where was he from?" Linda asked.

"Interesting question," Kyle replied. "I have no idea, but it's easy to find out—he booked the room online and his address will be part of that transaction. I think Denver. I seem to remember it when I went over the reservations."

"So he came from Denver to research his family history, or his genealogy ..."

"Something like that."

"... something like that, and he gets killed for his efforts."

"Obviously because of what he found out."

"Is it, Kyle? We don't know why he was killed, or even if he was. It could be suicide. Maybe he was sick and he came here to tie up loose ends."

"Before jumping off a bridge into the Delaware River? I don't see it, Linda. I'd bet the house he was murdered."

"In a town that sees a murder once every five years, maybe ten."

"And a day after Harold Summit was killed. I doubt that's a coincidence."

Returning to the Day Planner pages, Linda said, "So what else is there here to see?"

"There's a name and phone number to go with Paul," Kyle responded, pointing at a sheet from the contact section. "Paul Thibodeaux, with a local area code. I'm guessing that's who he had dinner with the first night he was here. It's in the calendar, and he'd told Patty he was going out to eat with an old friend."

"So Garland was from Lambertville?"

"I don't think so. I have no idea how he had a friend here, but there's an easy way to find out."

Kyle took the photocopy and walked over to the wall phone. In an age of smartphones and streaming television, they'd decided to still keep a landline for business purposes.

Linda finished her coffee while she watched Kyle make the

call.

"Hello?" Kyle said, nodding at Linda: he hadn't gotten a voicemail. "Is this Paul Thibodeaux? Yes, my name's Kyle Callahan. I own the bed and breakfast where Joseph Garland is staying ... *was* staying. Yes, it's been on the news. It's just that I believe he had dinner with you his first night here and I was wondering if we could speak in person."

He smiled at Linda and gave her a thumbs-up, feeling morbid for doing it under the circumstances but relieved Thibodeaux had agreed to meet them.

"An hour? That would be fine," he said, returning to the conversation. "I'll be with a friend of mine, her name's Linda. She's a retired detective from New Hope. No, sir, we're not the police. I can explain when we see you. Now what's your address?"

Linda hurried over with one of the sheets of paper. Kyle took a pen from a small box they kept near the phone and started writing.

CHAPTER 36

Under normal circumstances Gladys would enjoy being secluded in a room with Carol, despite her wife's incessant talking. She'd come to experience it as a pleasant white noise, reassuring in its annoyance. But these were not normal circumstances, and Carol's eerie calm just made Gladys more unnerved.

"What if they think I had something to do with his murder?" Gladys asked, for the tenth time by Carol's count. No amount of reassurance had convinced her that she was the last person anyone would suspect of killing a man.

Even patience as admirable as Carol's could be pressed to the breaking point. "Frankly, my dear, you're in no shape to harm anyone."

Gladys looked up at her from the bed where she'd been lying with her feet crossed at the ankles. "What's that supposed to mean?"

Carol had been sitting in a chair trying to read a book of neo-feminist poetry by one of the authors at the convention.

"It means you couldn't sneak up on a deaf elephant," Carol replied. "You're fifty pounds overweight, you walk with a thud, and you breathe like someone having an asthma attack."

"I'm asthmatic!" Gladys snapped.

It wasn't true. Gladys had been using her imaginary asthma as an excuse to avoid unwanted activity for years, usually involving walking longer than it took to get to a car.

"Why are you being mean to me?" Gladys asked.

The dynamic playing out between the women was one that rarely came out. Every now and then, when Carol had failed after several attempts to get Gladys to listen to reason, or simply to stop obsessing, Carol would say something blunt and truthful, and Gladys would become insecure and vulnerable, like a child whose bravado had been exposed as fear.

"I'm not being mean to you. I'm just trying to get through to you. There's nothing to worry about, and if you don't stop, you're going to have a stroke. I'm not ready to lose you, my dear. And think of it—if you die on me, Harold Summit will have stolen your ideas *and* your life."

Gladys was silent a moment, then said, "Well, when you put it that way."

She motioned for the welcome basket sitting on the coffee table. Carol put the poetry book down, got the basket and took it over to the bed, sitting beside Gladys as they started picking through the goodies, deciding which to eat.

"Turn on the TV," Gladys said, settling on a package of blueberry biscotti. "Let's see what's on."

Carol took the remote and turned on the TV just in time to catch a reporter a giving an update on a second death in the area, now suspected to be a homicide.

Gladys stopped eating, fascinated by the report.

Both women stared at the photograph of Joseph Garland being shown on the news.

A second murder, of a second guest, at the house they were staying at.

"Well, they can't blame me for this one," Gladys said.

"It's awful," Carol muttered. "Just awful."

Then, turning to her beloved, temperamental soulmate, Carol said, "What if someone's killing all the guests?"

Gladys dropped her biscotti on the bedspread, staring open-mouthed at her wife.

Scott wished he missed Harold more. He'd never been a widower before, and he wasn't sure how he was supposed to act or what he was supposed to feel, but surely a sense of loss was high on the list. He'd loved Harold ... had he not? He certainly had never imagined Harold's life ending in a muddy canal with a bullet to the back of his head. It was conjecture on his part, to be sure—he had no idea if Harold had been shot in the head or the back or the heart—but he'd watched enough television and read enough novels to know that's where most assassinated people were shot. "Execution style," they called it. But why would anyone execute an old writer of thrillers on the downslope of his career? And how long would it take for the transfer-on-death accounts to kick in?

Harold had resisted opening a joint bank account. He'd said there was no need for it, and he wasn't going to open one for sentimental reasons. They had a marriage license and that was enough, he'd said. They did not need joint accounts or both names on the deeds to their house or any of that. If Harold died before Scott, everything would go to him as his legally married husband. The question now for Scott was just how long that would take. He'd almost called their bank back in Los Angeles several times this morning, only to hang up when he decided it would look unseemly. He also didn't want any official record of having been too quick to secure any inheritance from Harold. There was a life insurance policy Scott knew better than to pursue for now. Each of them had them at Harold's insistence, but they always made the surviving spouse look suspicious if death had not been by natural causes. It had been hard for Scott to adjust so suddenly to having a deceased husband, and a murdered one at that, while still having to ensure his own ... comfort? Survival? That worked: everyone has to survive, and that meant calling a bank the day after his husband was killed, or going through Harold's phone ...

Where *was* Harold's phone? The police detective had not said anything about it. Harold hadn't answered when Scott called him a half dozen times after fleeing the conference reception. Maybe it was in the muddy canal, lodged in the dirt or sunk to the bottom. Scott assumed Hoyt would give him the phone eventually if the police had it. It wasn't a murder weapon. It was, however, a key to much of Harold's life. He'd kept everything on there, like the mini-computer it was meant to be. Contacts, passwords, account numbers. Scott made a note to ask, in the most delicate way possible, if they'd found Harold's phone and when he might get it, as a precious memento of their life together, of course.

Scott tried to decide if it would look bad for him to walk into town. He was hungry, and he'd eyed the cinnamon rolls at the coffee shop yesterday. Harold wasn't around to tell him he shouldn't be eating such things; he was already ten pounds overweight. In fact, Harold wasn't around to tell him anything, or to criticize him, or to belittle him in the subtle ways he'd been doing for five years. Harold would never make Scott feel inferior again. And when he'd arranged the inevitable memorial service back in L.A., attended by dozens, possibly hundreds, Scott would be sure to say how achingly he missed Harold's voice and his loving touch.

For now he wanted a sticky bun and a cappuccino. He slipped his wallet into his back pocket, fastened his phone holster to his belt, and left his room, adjusting his expression on the way out to erase any hint of a smile.

CHAPTER 37

"I've known Joseph for over forty years. *Knew* him, I should say, considering what's happened."

Paul Thibodeaux was a quiet and elegant man. Kyle felt a sense of regret at having intruded into his grief, but he was the only person he believed could give them any useful information. No one else, to their knowledge, knew who Joseph Garland was or why he may really have come to Lambertville. Kyle's belief that the personal lives of his houseguests were none of his business had run up against a need to find out why they were being murdered. With two of them found dead in the span of two days, he worried that a third was in the planning.

Thibodeaux lived alone in a house much too large for one elderly gentleman, and Kyle wondered if there had once been a brood of Thibodeauxs filling the large three story home, or if the man was simply a wealthy eccentric who preferred the company of empty rooms.

Linda continued to stand while Kyle had taken a seat at Thibodeaux's suggestion in an old, very overstuffed armchair. The man himself sat on a couch, arms on his knees as he leaned forward thinking about it all.

"I can't imagine anyone killing him. The news reports haven't said they did. Are you sure it wasn't an accident?"

Kyle glanced at Linda. "We're not sure of anything, Mr. Thibodeaux. Detective Sikorsky and I are just trying to get some information about Mr. Garland — why he was visiting, where he may have gone before ... well, you understand."

"Yes and no," said Thibodeaux. Looking at Linda, he added, "I thought you said the lady was retired."

"That's correct," Linda said. "I met Kyle during an investigation several years ago. We've become friends and I live nearby. He asked for my help."

Thibodeaux frowned. "I should think you'd ask the police for that."

"Oh, we will, absolutely," Kyle said quickly. "This is just preliminary. My husband and I own Passion House, the bed and

124

breakfast Mr. Garland was staying at, and we hoped to get some understanding of why he was here. He mentioned having dinner with you last Monday."

"Did he?" Garland's tone had become suspicious. "It was something he hadn't intended to tell anyone about—his presence here, I mean."

"Of course," said Kyle. "And he didn't. He simply mentioned having dinner out with a friend his first night at the house."

Kyle hoped Thibodeaux would not ask the obvious question: how did they know about *him*?

"Your name and address were on a notepad in his room," Linda said, attempting to head off any problem. "The housekeeper Patty found it and thought it might be important."

"Right, right," said Kyle. "That's how we knew to call you. And now that we're here ..."

"I might as well tell you what I know," Thibodeaux said, finishing the thought. "I see your point. Joseph is dead and it won't matter now. Will the police be asking me the same questions?"

"I'm sure they will, Mr. Thibodeaux," said Linda. "Our coming here could be a way of refreshing your memory."

He stared at her. "My memory is quite fine, Ms. Sikorsky."

Linda: "I didn't mean to—"

Thibodeaux cut her off with a wave. "Joseph was here to find out what happened to his nephew. His late wife's nephew, I should say. Kevin Lockland was Louise's brother's son. Joseph's nephew by marriage. It's really not complicated. The lineage, I mean."

"Of course not," said Kyle. His interest had spiked and he wanted to keep Thibodeaux focused. "What was Mr. Garland after?"

"Kevin! He wanted to know what happened to Kevin ... where he went, why he vanished, and *how*."

Linda moved closer. "Kevin was from Lambertville?"

"Oh, yes," said Thibodeaux. "And he was from here because of me. I introduced him to Melissa—that's his wife, or widow, whatever one is when one's spouse disappears—and I've felt so responsible for the past year."

"That's when Kevin left?" asked Kyle.

"You seem to be missing the point, young man."

Kyle had not been called a young man for quite a while. He smiled despite himself.

"Kevin Lockland did not leave. Joseph refused to believe that, and I agreed with him. Kevin would never simply go away and not tell anyone. It was true his marriage was in trouble, that was common knowledge and has caused more than a little malicious gossip, but it was an amicable separation."

"So they were separated?" asked Kyle.

Thibodeaux tilted his head up slightly and stared down his nose, annoyed.

"Did I not just say that?"

"You did," said Kyle. "My apology. I was just surprised."

"As were we all when Kevin disappeared. He and Melissa never stopped getting along, they just grew apart. It's impossible she would have harmed him, and just as impossible he would have vanished off the face of the earth. But that's exactly what seems to have happened, and Joseph was determined to uncover the truth."

"So why the secrecy?" Linda asked.

Thibodeaux thought about it a moment. "He's dead now, isn't he? And you believe he was murdered for what he discovered. I think that answers your question."

Kyle knew he was right. Whatever precautions Joseph Garland had taken to keep his presence in town a secret, someone had found out he was here and why. Was it the same someone who'd killed Harold Summit, Kyle wondered. How could they possibly be connected?

"I believe it had something to do with that bank," Thibodeaux said, as if reading Kyle's mind.

"Which bank is that, Mr. Thibodeaux?" Linda asked, though she and Kyle both anticipated the answer.

"River Valley, where Kevin used to work," Thibodeau replied. "And so did Harold Summit. They both moved on after the bank was acquired, but Joseph was convinced his nephew's disappearance had some connection to their time there."

Kyle felt his heart pounding. They were getting somewhere quickly.

"Please, sir," he said. "Tell us what you know."

"Coffee, then," Thibodeaux said, standing from the couch. "If you want my time, then I shall have some of yours. It's a big house, as you can see, and I've stopped keeping cats. They'd outlive me at this point, and that's not a nice thing to do to a pet. So it's me and the sound of my footsteps echoing around this old place. I'll make some coffee, dig out some crackers or something, and tell you a story. I'm sure you don't mind."

Kyle looked at his watch, and said, "Of course not, Mr. Thibodeaux. We'd very much enjoy spending some time with you."

"All things considered," Thibodeaux said, as he shuffled down a hallway toward what Kyle assumed was a kitchen.

"Yes, all things considered," Kyle replied.

Linda took a seat on the couch, resigned to giving the old gentleman the time he wanted in exchange for the information they needed.

CHAPTER 38

Kyle sat in the passenger seat of Linda's car while they talked over what Thibodeaux had told them. There'd been no reason to take two vehicles, so they'd left Kyle's in the driveway of Passion House.

"That was quite a story," Linda said, staring out the front window. A woman walking two dogs up the sidewalk had caught her attention. They'd seen a squirrel and gotten excited, yanking the poor woman into a yard.

"You mean that Kevin Lockland embezzled money from a bank?" Kyle asked. "Or that his wife had nothing to do with his disappearance?"

Thibodeaux had shocked them with a tale of theft on a large scale, an unsolved crime, a disappearance, and a sizable helping of town gossip.

"Both, I think."

"Maybe they're connected. Maybe she knew he'd stolen the money."

"And she knew where he'd kept it hidden over the years."

Lockland had left River Valley Bank fifteen years ago when it was gobbled up by a larger competitor. Exactly why he'd left was unknown for now, but where he'd gone to was not a secret. He'd taken a job with Pennsylvania Savings and Trust in New Hope. That's where he'd been since then, until his abrupt departure from everyone's life. According to Paul Thibodeaux, Lockland was under investigation for stealing either fifty thousand or a quarter million dollars, depending on whom you asked. His wife had been questioned several times, something Thibodeaux knew because she was his niece, but no proof of her involvement in the embezzlement or in her husband's disappearance had ever been established.

"Maybe they spent it all and she wanted more," Kyle said. "You can get used to luxury. A life insurance policy could provide some quick cash."

"If it was paid out," Linda replied. "No body, no death. It's also possible she knew the walls were closing in, so she helped her husband ..."

"Who she was amicably separated from ..."

"Conveniently vanish."

"Willingly or unwillingly," Kyle added darkly. "But why bring attention to herself that way?"

"Maybe because he *was* planning to leave, with whatever money he still had, and without her."

"What if that's what really happened and he's living on a beach somewhere with a suitcase of hundred dollar bills under his bed?"

The possibility that Kevin Lockland was still alive had been an obvious one, but dismissed out of hand by Joseph Garland and his friend Paul Thibodeaux. Both men were convinced Kevin had met a bad end. That was why Garland had come to Lambertville, and the most likely reason he was dead.

"Let's go," Kyle said, fastening his seat belt.

They'd decided before leaving Thibodeaux to his large empty house that the next stop would be the Carlisle Gallery, a long-established art gallery on Coryell Street where Melissa Lockland worked. It was among the oldest galleries in town, and Thibodeaux told them Melissa had worked there part-time for the past several years.

"Do you think Harold Summit was in on it?" Linda asked, starting the car.

"I don't know," replied Kyle. "But both men are deceased, and both men worked at River Valley Bank years ago. There's got to be a connection."

As Linda pulled away from the curb, she said, "Kevin Lockland was never charged. If he embezzled all this money, why wasn't he in jail?"

"Hopefully his wife can shed some light on that," Kyle replied. "Whatever her responsibility is in any of this, she's a key to unlocking the mystery."

"Myster*ies*," Linda corrected. "I believe we're looking at more than one."

"You're right, as usual," Kyle said. "That's why I needed you on this. I think, too, that solving one puzzle will lead to solving all the others."

Linda nodded as they pulled into the street and drove away.

CHAPTER 39

Justin never expected it to come to this. How could he? Just two days ago he was happily employed at a bed and breakfast in a town he loved and had grown up in. He was young, attractive, and skilled enough in the ways of the world to have gotten what he'd wanted most of his life. Fame and fortune had eluded him, sure, but he'd never sought those things. He was a man of the moment, and he'd had hundreds of spectacular moments, many of them involving men who had appreciated his gifts and responded with some of their own. Even the backpack he'd stuffed with an extra pair of jeans, three T-shirts, socks and underwear, had been purchased for him on a trip to New York City with someone named Richard ... or Randall, or Robert, he couldn't remember exactly. They'd spent a night at the Marriot Marquis in Times Square. Robert (or Randall, or Richard) had taken him to see his first Broadway musical, and the next day they'd driven back with a stop at McDonald's. The man never contacted Justin again, but like anyone with a healthy ego, Justin did not attribute this to any fault of his own. He'd assumed he was simply too much to handle, too *hot*, and Randall (or Robert, or Richard) had severed their flimsy ties to save himself from heartbreak and frustration. Justin Stritch belonged to no one, and those with designs on him soon learned it.

He'd taken a last, long look around his room at Passion House. It hadn't been much, not large at all, but it had been home for the past few months. He'd grown very comfortable there, and with the others — Kyle and Danny, and even Patty, who'd treated him like the type of mother people should have but don't want. She'd kept an eye on him, and while he hadn't liked it, he had appreciated being looked after. His own parents hadn't cared much where he went or what happened to him, and he'd not spoken to his mother since he'd walked out of their house the last time six years ago.

He would have preferred taking his suitcase, but that would be too obvious. Even if he made it past Patty downstairs, someone would see him rolling it up the street. With a backpack, they would just tell the police they'd seen him walking into town, a familiar sight most days. A lot of people knew Justin, even some of the husbands in their more secretive moments, and it wasn't unusual to spot him walking through the neighborhoods. They might remember a backpack, but that's all it was. Other than that, they would just see him strolling toward Bridge Street in his windbreaker, the backpack over his shoulder and a smile on his face as he waved at one or two of them. "Morning, Mrs. Greenleaf," he'd say as he walked past her house, and, "Summer's coming, Mrs. Leeland," to the woman tending her front flower garden. Just another day ... and the last one he'd spend in Lambertville, possibly forever.

He walked to Bridge Street and stood on the corner, looking around. He would miss this city. He hoped to come back when things were resolved. He'd keep his eye on the news from Sammy's place in Chelsea. Sammy Crocker had been a running buddy of Justin's who'd made it big in New York, if you considered holding down a steady job and paying for a studio apartment big. At least he's not living in a third floor closet in someone else's house, Justin thought, as he checked his watch. The Trans-Bridge bus would be there in ten minutes. It was an easy way to get from Manhattan to Lambertville, New Hope, and Doylestown. Some people even commuted, but Justin thought spending nearly two hours each way on a bus was a horrible way to get to work. Sammy had moved three years ago and never come back, not once. Justin had gone to see him a few times, and Sammy had been happy to hear from him last night. Justin suggested a surprise visit, and Sammy thought it was a great idea. Justin would wait a while to tell Sammy he wasn't going back to Lambertville. He knew Sammy would be okay with that, at least for a few days, and by then they might have caught the killer. Maybe Kyle and Danny would take him back. Or maybe he'd do what Sammy had done and make it big in New York City. For someone like Justin, the options seemed limitless. He'd believed that all his life. He'd had to.

He got to the bus stop by the gas station just in time to see the bus turning the corner toward him. He was confident no one had seen him, and if they had, so what? New York City was big, with about eight million places to hide.

CHAPTER 40

The Carlisle was one of the few galleries in town Kyle had never been to. He avoided it and he knew why: the gallery specialized in photography, a passion of Kyle's that had waned but that had once been central to his life. So central, in fact, that it had led indirectly to his involvement with murder and his relationship with Linda. It had been an image of the empty blue pool at Pride Lodge that had caught his attention one weekend, a stark and beautiful visual of the pool bottom with leaves blown into a corner as if they were huddling together against the wind. He'd reached for the camera on a strap around his neck and taken a photograph that affected his life in ways he could never have imagined. The picture was eventually featured in his first exhibit at the Katherine Pride Gallery in Manhattan. Teddy Pembroke had been found dead in that pool, and Katherine Pride herself was almost murdered a year later. Time marched on, and Kyle finally found himself in a therapist's office grappling with having killed a man. At the same time, he'd lost any desire to ever take another photograph. He'd tried to revive it, to reignite his love for the out-of-focus hallway and the unguarded expression, but it had left him and never returned. So when he and Danny first walked past the Carlisle and Danny suggested they go inside, Kyle declined. Photography, and galleries that featured it, were not for him.

They pulled into a parking spot almost directly in front of the Carlisle. Linda had never been there, either, which wasn't surprising. She'd been a cop, and then a shop owner. Nothing in her life said artistic snapshots.

"According to Thibodeaux she works on Fridays," Kyle said when they'd gotten out of the car.

"You do the talking if she's here," Linda replied. "I'll stand back and chime in if I'm needed."

"You're always needed, Detective."

Linda moaned. "Don't start calling me that again, please. I'm not coming out of retirement for this. I'm just your support."

"Understood."

They walked into the gallery and Kyle was immediately taken

back to his days as an aspiring photographer. The main room was sparse, as it would be in an art gallery, with off-white walls offering dozens of meticulously shot and framed photographs. A woman came into the room, having somehow been alerted to their entrance (Kyle had not heard a buzzer or bell of any kind). She looked older than Kyle had imagined Melissa Lockland to be, and he wondered if this was someone else.

"May I help you?" the woman asked.

She was wearing creased beige slacks, a light blue blouse under a slightly darker blue sweater, and deck shoes. Her hair, full, curly and half-gray, was tied loosely back.

"We're looking for Melissa Lockland," Kyle said, offering her a smile he hoped didn't look too forced.

She stared at him a moment, apparently realizing they weren't here for the pictures on the walls.

"That's me," she said. "And you are?"

Kyle did not extend his hand. Something told him she would ignore it, and he preferred to avoid the embarrassment.

"Kyle Callahan," he said. "I run Passion House Bed and Breakfast. You may have heard of us."

She gave no indication she had.

"And this is Linda Sikorsky, a friend of mine."

Kyle refrained from saying Linda had once been a detective; it was a card he played when he had to, but the timing was not right. He wanted to establish for Lockland that they were not here as adversaries or interrogators, and he may not mention Linda's previous profession at all.

"Are you looking for something for your home? Or your business, perhaps?" Lockland asked, trying to veer them away from her and onto the display of photographs.

"No, Mrs. Lockland," Linda said, having decided it was time to say something. "We were hoping to talk to you about your husband."

"He's not here."

"We know that," Kyle said. "We also know he disappeared a six months ago."

"Who did you say sent you?" she asked.

"No one," Kyle replied. "We spoke to Paul Thibodaux." He could tell she was surprised by that information. "You see, Joseph Garland is a guest at my bed and breakfast ... *was* a guest. You may have heard about what happened to him on the news this morning."

"Come in the back please," Lockland said.

She walked to the front window, flipped the sign to "Closed" and locked the door. A moment later she led them to the back room where a small seating area had been set up for visitors to the gallery. She took a chair and motioned for them to do the same.

"I don't know what my uncle told you, but I didn't know Joe Garland well at all. He was Kevin's relative, and they weren't close anymore. I saw the news, yes, but it didn't say anything about what happened to him, only that they'd found his body in the river."

"They weren't close anymore?" asked Linda, trying to stay focused.

"It goes back a ways. Joe and Paul were instrumental in my meeting Kevin, but it wasn't more involved than that. Elise – that was Joe's wife – was very fond of Kevin. He was her favorite nephew. But once Kevin and I were married we only saw them a couple times on trips out West. Joe had never been to Lambertville, as far as I know."

"He seemed very determined to find out what became of Kevin," Kyle said.

Lockland shrugged. "Probably from some dedication he felt to Elise. She died six months ago not knowing what happened to my husband. None of us does."

Kyle and Linda glanced at each other, a look not lost on Melissa Lockland.

"I had nothing to do with Kevin vanishing, if that's what you think. And it's a fair way to describe it. He left, or was taken away, or *whatever* happened to him, with nothing but the clothes he was wearing, his wallet and his phone. Once he was gone, there was never any indication he was even still alive. No bank withdrawals, no phone calls, nothing. They tried to trace his phone, with pings and that kind of thing, but it's like he'd turned it off ..."

"Or someone else had," Linda said.

"Yes, that's the most likely scenario. I know the police think I had something to do with it, but I did not, and they've never come up with anything to suggest I had."

"What about the bank?" Kyle asked.

"What *about* the bank?" Lockland replied, an edge of anger in her voice. "If you're talking about the funds that were embezzled, Kevin didn't do that."

"You know this for a fact?" asked Linda.

Lockland stared at her, and Kyle sensed they were reaching a point where the woman might tell them to leave.

Leaning forward, Melissa said, "I know my husband was innocent. Whatever his faults were, Kevin was not a thief. The investigation is ongoing, if I'm correct. There were a half dozen people at the bank who could have stolen money from them. You'd have to talk to the branch manager, or the police, anyone but me. I took a polygraph, did Paul tell you that?"

It had not come out in their conversation with Thibodeaux, and Kyle wondered if the man had left it out on purpose. Maybe he'd come to dislike his niece, or he thought she was involved despite any results of a polygraph test.

"I passed, needless to say. I had nothing to do with my husband's disappearance."

"Estranged husband," Linda said.

Lockland stared at her. "We never stopped being friends," she said coolly. "We just weren't working as a married couple. It happens."

. Kyle thought the conversation was coming to an end. He was prepared to leave having learned next to nothing, when Melissa said, "I also know Kevin was threatened."

Kyle was startled by the information. "Threatened?" he said. "In what way?"

"Emails," Lockland explained. "Three or four of them he got in the month before he disappeared."

"Who sent them?" asked Linda.

"That's the problem—we don't know. The police even thought Kevin had sent them to himself somehow, or that I'd done it to throw them off track. It's all been horrible, enough to make me want to leave Lambertville. I still might."

"Do you have the emails?" Kyle asked.

"Not on me," Lockland replied dryly. "They traced the IP address, by the way. The mails came from an internet cafe in Philadelphia. Anyone could have set up an email account and sent them."

"What did the emails say?"

"Something about justice," Lockland said.

"Justice?" said Linda.

"Yes. 'Justice is patient, merciless and final.' Those are the words I remember. The other emails were variations of the same—someone held Kevin responsible for something they believed he'd done, and they planned to make him pay."

"Something from his past," Kyle said. "Patience means the person had taken their time."

"Or *is* taking their time," Linda added.

"Whatever it meant," said Lockland, "Kevin was gone a month later and no trace of him has been found. Joe came to town to try and find out what happened, and it appears to have gotten him killed. I think maybe I should go somewhere. This is not a safe place."

Kyle thought about that a moment. Lambertville had seemed among the safest places they could live, but maybe Melissa Lockland was right. Things certainly didn't turn out well here for Harold Summit, Joseph Garland, and apparently Kevin Lockland.

"Did you know Harold Summit?" Kyle asked, now convinced there was a connection between them all.

"Before he was a famous author, yes," said Lockland. "He was Kevin's boss at River Valley Bank."

"His boss?"

"Mr. Summit was the assistant branch manager. Kevin was third man on the totem pole. He handled mortgages and loans, and Summit approved them. That's about all I know of it. Kevin didn't talk much about his work. It was a bank, what's to say?"

"Do you know if anyone from those days is still around?" asked Linda.

"You mean since one of them can't be found and the other one's dead?"

"I didn't—"

"It's okay. Those are just the facts. But yes, Dean Robbins is still around. He works at Pennsylvania Savings across the river. He got Kevin to move there after River Valley was acquired. They'd all worked together. He's the only person I can think of. Now if you don't mind, I need to get back to business.

Lockland stood up, prompting Kyle and Linda to do the same.

"I'm sorry I couldn't be more helpful. I know that sounds

untruthful, but it's not. Having a reputation as a murderer who got away with it is not all it's cracked up to be."

"I can see why you'd consider leaving town," Linda said. "Although I hope you don't. Then whoever is doing this would have another victim."

She walked them to the front of the gallery, turned the sign back to "Open" and held the door for them as they left.

"I hope you find my husband," she said, as they turned to walk to the car. "We were close to reconciling. Kevin had his issues, but he was a good man. He didn't deserve whatever happened to him."

Kyle just nodded and waved. He knew in his bones that Kevin Lockland would not be found alive, if he was found at all. Someone was killing people connected to Kevin's past, and so far they had a perfect record.

CHAPTER 41

Gladys had not been in a police station since her protest days fifty years ago fighting the patriarchy and the Vietnam War. She'd been a livewire then, and known for throwing a flame or two.

"Those were the days," Gladys mused.

"What, Dear?"

Carol was sitting next to her in the decidedly uncomfortable chairs the station offered for visitors. Gladys had once commented that waiting room chairs, like theater chairs and most others provided for public use, seemed to have been designed by small people, for small people. One of the reasons she'd disliked her few trips to New York City was because she couldn't possibly fit into a subway seat if anyone sat beside her. It was as embarrassing as it was infuriating.

"Nothing," Gladys said, staring at the young woman at the front desk. Her gaydar had tingled and she suspected the woman had a wife or a girlfriend somewhere. "I was just thinking about the last time I'd been in custody."

"You're not in custody," Carol said, sounding alarmed that Gladys would say such a thing. Maybe it was a sign of declining cognitive function, or just Gladys's peculiar phrasing.

Gladys harrumphed. "I know that. But I was arrested a few times in my youth and I was reflecting on it, that's all."

"Did you want to be arrested again?" Carol asked.

"What a ridiculous thing to say. It's also something you should only say under your breath. We're in a police station, Carol, about to give statements in a homicide investigation. This is the last place I want to be."

It was true. Gladys had been expressing her regret about the trip ever since Sergeant Hoyt showed up the night before. She'd berated herself aloud a dozen times for letting something as pointless as ruining a man's career bring her all the way to New Jersey. She'd made her splash, getting Harold Summit very wet in the process. Unfortunately, any drop in his book sales would be more than made up for when people started buying them because he'd been murdered. *Murder Mystery Author Dies in Mysterious*

Murder. She could see the stories now. Of course, Summit didn't really write mysteries. His oeuvre was the thriller, with his protagonist Connor Dark's life always about to end at the hand of some cunning villain. But the media wouldn't let something as trivial as a genre stop them from writing salacious and overly clever headlines.

Gladys was thinking how much she'd rather be sitting on her couch at home petting Lulubear, their elderly Calico cat being looked after by a neighbor, when Sergeant Hoyt suddenly appeared in front of them, wearing typical office clothes and a sport coat that gave no hint of what he did for a living.

"Good morning, ladies, and thank you for coming."

"Morning," Carol said, sheepishly. The only authority she was used to being in the presence of was Gladys. Police were foreign to her except for the few times she'd been stopped for a traffic violation.

"Good morning, Lieutenant," Gladys said.

"Sergeant," Hoyt corrected her. "Now, who would like to go first?"

Carol seemed flummoxed. "I thought you'd interrogate us together."

"I'm not interrogating anyone, Ms. Dupree."

Gladys was impressed that he'd remembered her wife's name. She answered Hoyt by standing up and nodding toward a corridor of offices, assuming that's where they'd be going.

"After you, Sergeant," she said.

Hoyt motioned for Gladys to lead the way. "Right down the hallway, please." Turning back to Carol, he added, "Twenty minutes, maybe less. Just to go over what you told me last night."

Carol smiled anxiously. She was alone in a police station far from home. Two men, who'd both been staying in the same house with them, were now dead, and her wife had made a scene accusing one of them of a crime not much lower on the scandal scale than matricide: stealing her intellectual property. If that wasn't motive, Carol didn't know what was. She looked at the woman behind the front desk, getting not so much as a glance in return. She wanted to leave, right that very moment, to grab their things, get in their car and drive out of Lambertville as fast as the speed limit allowed. But running was not an option. They had nothing to run from. They had done nothing wrong. They had only to tell the truth as they knew it and let the good sergeant do his job.

Gladys had never been interviewed by a homicide detective before, or by any policeman for that matter. Having gotten most of her experience with police stations from watching crime dramas on television, she'd expected to be put in a temperature-controlled room, in a deliberately ill-fitting chair, possibly with a leg chain attached to it, and grilled mercilessly until she broke down and told them what they wanted to know. Instead she was in a small conference room that looked like any she might encounter in an office large enough to have one.

"May I get you some coffee?" Hoyt asked, after pulling a chair out for Gladys to sit.

"No, thank you," she replied. "I'd like to be done here as soon as possible."

Hoyt smiled. "I'd like that, too."

He took a seat and adjusted a digital recorder on the table between them. Gladys hadn't noticed it at first. Hoyt then removed his notepad from his jacket pocket and flipped through to find the notations he'd made when they'd spoken at Passion House.

As he appeared to search his notes, he asked casually, "I understand you didn't get along with Harold Summit. Is that correct?"

He hadn't known the night before about her public accusation against Summit—and they hadn't told him. Gladys hoped it wasn't material to his investigation, and she wasn't about to make it that way if Hoyt didn't need the information. Someone had obviously told him, and he was asking her about it as if it was a passing thought, when she knew it was not.

"I didn't know him," Gladys said. "I only met the man after we checked in."

"Not knowing him isn't the same as not knowing *of* him, and I think you did, Ms. Finch."

He found the pages he was looking for, flipped the pad open to them and set it on the table, raising his eyes to Gladys as he did.

"You can tell me," he said. "Being angry with someone doesn't mean you had anything to do with his death."

Gladys was flustered, an emotional state that was foreign to her. She usually did the flustering.

"He stole my story," she said.

Hoyt waited a moment, and Gladys got the distinct impression he already knew what she was about to tell him. It reminded her of something she'd always heard about prosecutors: they never ask questions they don't already have the answers to.

"It's a long story," Gladys said, feeling deflated and exposed.

"We're in no hurry," said Hoyt.

"You may not be," Gladys replied. She then took a deep breath and began telling him the sad chain of events that led from her submitting a short story to an obscure magazine, to Harold Summit's wealth and success, and finally to Gladys exposing Summit at the writers conference just hours before someone found him dead in a canal.

And all that was before Hoyt ever mentioned the death of Joseph Garland.

CHAPTER 42

Scott couldn't help himself. He'd been compulsively dialing Harold's phone number hoping someone would answer it. That would mean it was turned on and the police could trace it. Sergeant Hoyt had told him Harold's phone was missing—he'd thought perhaps Scott had it for some reason, and it was now evidence in a murder investigation. Scott told him he did not possess Harold's phone, why would he, and he immediately concluded it had been taken by the killer. But what for? Was there something on Harold's phone that could implicate the person who'd murdered him? Maybe it was the hookup app he'd downloaded and thought Scott didn't know about. Maybe that's what got him killed, arranging casual sex with a stranger who then robbed him, or tried to rob him, and shot him. Scott knew Harold was the type to resist. If someone had wanted his wallet, they would have gotten a stern talking-to with it. Most people don't like to be lectured, and some of them may shoot you for it. Or perhaps he'd treated an anonymous trick to a line of his precious cocaine and the man wanted more ... or wanted all of it, so he put a bullet in Harold and ran off with the silver case. Scott had not told Hoyt about Harold's private stash and Hoyt had not mentioned it, or anything else that might have been found with the body. Harold's death in a canal was lurid enough; he didn't need his memory soiled by details of drugs and sex.

Scott had decided to walk to the police station. After looking it up on Google maps he knew it wasn't far, just over to Main Street and a half-mile up the road. He'd considered driving, but the last time he'd been in the car was with Harold, and he didn't want the memories. He was still grappling with his emotions, veering from grieving husband to surviving spouse with benefits. Harold's Social Security would be much more than his, too, when he finally reached retirement age. He'd have to look into it.

He'd glanced out his window just before leaving the house and had seen Justin walking up the street with a backpack. He'd wondered where the young man was going. It wasn't in the same direction as the police station, so there wouldn't be much chance of running into him. He hadn't mentioned Justin's and Harold's little powwow in the kitchen during breakfast. It had slipped his mind in the shock of being told Harold was dead. But he would certainly bring it up today. Any information that could help — and direct the good sergeant away from Scott himself — was important information. He had no idea if Justin Stritch was capable of murder. He knew nothing about the man, except that he had no scruples and that he'd surely planned to meet up with Harold at some point during their stay at Passion House. Had he managed to rendezvous with Harold? And had it ended with a gunshot? Scott would leave that up the good detective to investigate.

He hadn't seen the other house guests since breakfast and he wondered if any of them had checked out. He wasn't privy to what Hoyt had told the others, but he knew some of them had been instructed to stay in town. The lesbian couple, most certainly. Gladys Finch had a grudge, and she'd leveled an accusation against Harold that was stunning enough to put her on the short list of suspects. But the others? Maybe they'd been cleared and had already left. He didn't know or particularly care, and the dour housemaid, Patty, had vanished after breakfast. The woman had a way of coming and going so quietly it was unnerving. Scott was happy not to see her when he left the house and headed toward Main Street. The more he thought about it, the more things he had to tell Sergeant Hoyt. Some of it was misdirection, but all of it was the truth, depending on whom you asked.

CHAPTER 43

Pennsylvania Savings and Trust was among a handful of small banks that had not been gobbled up by the giants in the industry. Located in New Hope at the corner of W. Randolph and Main Street, the bank recently celebrated its fiftieth anniversary, with signage in all six branches letting its customers know they were its reason for being. "Fifty Years of Serving You" posters with stock images of happy citizens still hung in the windows, two months after the actual anniversary.

Kyle wasn't used to taking a car across the bridge to Pennsylvania. There was no free parking in town anymore, so he and Danny always parked on a side street in Lambertville and walked over. Linda found a spot in front of the bank and paid at the parking kiosk.

"We should have called first," Linda said, glancing at the bank entrance.

"It's a short trip," replied Kyle. "If he's not here, we didn't waste much time."

They walked into the bank, finding what Kyle expected in a small operation like this: two tellers looking busy behind a counter (tellers never look like they have nothing to do, Kyle thought), a woman who appeared to be in her late thirties or early forties dressed in a pantsuit and sitting at a desk, and an older gentleman in a small office to the side—the only enclosed space Kyle could see.

When the woman realized they weren't going to a teller, she stood up from the desk.

"May I help you?" she asked. The name plate by her phone said Greta Whitman.

Linda stepped forward, putting out her hand. "Greta, hello. Do you remember me?"

Greta stopped and looked at Linda for a moment, trying to place her. "Of course! You're Officer Sikorsky."

Linda had been well known in town during her years with the police force. Her wife had been a fixture, too, having sold real estate in a market that only got hotter over the years. Linda hadn't seen Greta since she'd been a beat cop long ago. Greta wasn't even aware that she'd become a detective before retiring.

"I'm not with the police anymore," Linda said.

Greta frowned. "Oh, I hope nothing happened."

"Not at all, Greta. I'm retired. I live in New Jersey now, over in Kingwood with my wife Kirsten McClellan."

If the mention of having a wife surprised Greta she didn't show it.

"This is my friend, Kyle Callahan," Linda said.

"Pleased to meet you," said Kyle.

"We're looking into something," added Linda.

"A police matter?" Greta said, lowering her voice. "But that's a silly question, you just said you're retired."

"I am, but, well ..."

"I own a bed and breakfast in Lambertville," Kyle interjected. "We had a guest staying with us." He left out which guest he was referring to—Joseph Garland or Harold Summit—and the fact they were both dead. "To make a long story short, we were hoping Dean Robbins was here. We'd like to speak with him if he is."

Greta seemed perplexed by the request. She glanced at the office and the man inside. "He's here. Let me tell him you'd like to talk to him."

She disappeared into the office and began conversing with Robbins. Linda peered at him, wondering why she'd never met him. But there were many people she met only in the process of investigating a crime. Pennsylvania Savings had not had a robbery in her time on the force, and until now no murders had been connected to it in any way.

Greta stepped back out and waved Kyle and Linda over. A moment later she excused herself and left them alone with Robbins, who'd stood up from his desk and offered his hand to each of them.

"Dean Robbins," he said. "I'm the branch manager here. How may I help you?"

Robbins was wearing what Kyle called corporate drag: slacks, white shirt, tie, with a beige sport coat draped over the back of his chair. His face had enough lines to tell Kyle he was probably in his upper sixties, and he had an easy smile he offered to them as he motioned for everyone to sit.

"You look familiar," Robbins said to Linda, searching his memory while he studied her face.

"Linda Sikorsky," she replied. "I was with the police in New Hope. Twenty years."

"Ah, well, I live in Doylestown. I didn't spend much time at the police station before I worked here!" he said, laughing lightly. "What can I do for you?"

Kyle stepped in. "My name's Kyle Callahan. My husband and I own Passion House Bed and Breakfast in Lambertville."

Robbins's smile faded. "The one on the news?" he said. "Those dead men?"

"That's us, unfortunately. It's also why Linda and I are here. One of those men, Joseph Garland, was the uncle of Kevin Lockland. I understand he worked here."

"Before disappearing," Robbins said. "Yes, he was our loan officer for a number of years. Is this concerning the missing money?"

Kyle didn't want the conversation to get diverted into speculation about who may or may not have embezzled funds from the bank.

"Not at all," Kyle said.

"The investigation is ongoing, by the police and by Pennsylvania Savings."

Kyle wondered how long an investigation like that could take, given how small the branch was.

"It's certainly not someone here," Robbins said, as if reading Kyle's mind. "With electronic systems, something like that can be done from anywhere, even outside the bank. Kevin was never found to have committed any wrongdoing."

"So why kill him?" Linda asked.

The bluntness of it surprised Kyle. He and Linda had not suggested Lockland was dead, although he'd come to that conclusion himself.

"Kevin's dead?" Robbins said, startled.

"Sadly, that's what we suspect," Kyle said quickly. "But we have no evidence. That's why we're here, Mr. Robbins. To ask you some questions."

"About Kevin."

"About his time at River Valley Bank when you were both there."

Robbins was surprised. "That was, what, fifteen years ago?"

"At least," Linda said. "We understand he worked there with Harold Summit, and yourself."

Robbins leaned back in his chair, thinking about what they'd just said.

"That's correct. Harold was the assistant manager, I was the senior officer, and Kevin oversaw loans and mortgages. Harold left to be a writer — a good decision or a terrible one, considering how it ended. I moved over to this bank, and a few years later I encouraged Kevin to join us."

"You were unhappy at River Valley?" asked Kyle.

"Yes and no. Let's just say I needed a change, and we knew an acquisition was coming. I had no desire to work for a faceless conglomerate. Pennsylvania Savings is small but healthy, we won't be eaten by a bigger fish anytime soon."

Kyle leaned up and rested his arm on the desk. "I think — *we* think — there's a connection between the three men and that it has to do with River Valley Bank. Did they work together, Kevin and Harold?"

"Well, yes," said Robbins. "Anything Kevin was doing with loans and mortgages had to go past Harold. He was Kevin's boss, basically, and he had approval."

"Over who got a loan and who didn't?" asked Linda.

Robbins nodded. "Mortgages, too."

Kyle thought a moment, then asked, "What about who *didn't* get one?"

"A loan or a mortgage?"

"Either. Did Kevin have to get Harold's approval to turn someone down?"

Robbins appeared to consider his words before answering.

"Yes, he did. Once in a while, though not often, Kevin wanted to say no to someone looking for a loan — business loan, line of credit, a mortgage — and Harold would overrule him."

"Because the person was connected in some way," Linda said. It was not a question.

Robbins sighed. "Yes. It happens now and then. No one really got money they shouldn't have, and as far as I knew there was never any scandal, but sometimes it's 'you scratch my back and I'll scratch yours.' Strictly business, and perfectly legal."

"Was there ever anyone who got turned down and wasn't

happy about it?" Kyle asked.

He could tell by Linda's expression she was following his logic.

"Who is ever happy about being denied money, Mr. Callahan?"

"I mean *really* unhappy about it."

"I think I know what you're getting at, but this was at least fifteen years ago. Why would anyone wait this long to harm these men? And over what, a bank loan?"

"'Justice is patient, merciless and final,'" Kyle said, quoting the email Melissa Lockland had told them about.

"Pardon me?"

"Was there anyone who was especially upset?" Linda said, trying to keep them on track.

Robbins spread his hands. "I really don't know. Not that I can remember. But I know one person who might."

That got Kyle's attention. He sat back in his chair.

"Polly Bryson," Robbins said. "She was the branch manager when we were all there. Everybody's boss. She's retired now."

"Do you know where we can find her?" asked Kyle.

"I do, actually. We're Facebook friends. She lives in a retirement community outside town."

"Assisted living?"

"God no! She's not that old. And she's Polly. She's not going to let anyone assist her with anything. It's a development for people over fifty-five. I'm thinking of moving there myself eventually. Nice place, lots to do."

"Would you mind sharing her contact information with us?" Linda asked.

"As long as it's okay with her," Robbins said. "As a matter of fact, let's give her a call right now."

He picked up the phone on his desk and dialed.

Ten minutes later Kyle and Linda were back in the car, heading toward Hillsdale Estates.

CHAPTER 44

Sitting across from Sergeant Hoyt in the same conference room Gladys and Carol had been interviewed in just an hour earlier, Scott felt like a character in some hack writer's police procedural. It didn't help that Hoyt was so attractive. Scott was single now, regardless how he got that way, and he was having a hard time not staring at the detective.

"So you went to this reception," Hoyt said, prompting Scott to continue while he took notes.

The recorder was running again, and Scott wondered why he needed to write things down in addition to recording them. Maybe, he thought, it was just Hoyt's method, or maybe it was faster this way when he needed to go back over their conversation—he didn't have to scroll through the audiotape listening for the important points.

"I did," Scott said. He'd been shifting in his seat for the past twenty minutes and hoped Hoyt didn't take it as a sign of anything but discomfort, certainly not as an indication of guilt. "They were not nice to me."

Hoyt looked up from his notepad. "Who is 'they'?"

"The people at the writers conference. Not all of them, of course. I wasn't there long enough to meet more than the few who made it very clear I wasn't any more welcome than Harold had been."

Scott wasn't a mind reader, but he guessed the detective already had much of the information he was giving him. He knew the unpleasant Gladys Finch, whose books he would never read, had already been to the police station, along with her wife. Scott had run into them when they'd returned to the house, and Carol had cheerily told him they'd just been interrogated. He thought it seemed like a game to her, with death behind Door Number Three.

"Do you know why they were unwelcoming to Mr. Summit?"

Another question he knows the answer to, thought Scott.

"That awful woman who's staying at Passion House with us—with *me*—accused him of plagiarism. Can you imagine?

Harold Summit *stealing someone else's writing*? It's ridiculous."

"You're referring to Gladys Finch?"

"What other awful woman is there?" Scott said, testily. "She was rude to Harold the first time we met, and she stayed rude. Then she accused him of literary theft, which for writers is among the worst crimes imaginable."

"And then someone killed him."

Scott was startled by the statement. He'd considered the possibility that Harold was murdered as an act of revenge, but who would do something like that, and why? If the old bat Finch was going to kill him, why tell everyone by accusing him of plagiarism in a room full of witnesses? He still thought robbery was the most likely motive, but it wasn't his job to determine who murdered Harold or why.

"Yes," Scott replied, deflated. "And then someone killed him." After a moment he added, "Probably the person who has his phone."

Hoyt wrote a quick note and looked up at Scott. "We've subpoenaed the phone records and expect to have that this afternoon. Is there anything on there we should know about?"

Scott thought it was an odd question, almost a trap of some kind. Or was Hoyt giving him the opportunity to come clean, as he saw it, and confess?

"Not that I know of," Scott replied. "Harold was very possessive of his phone. I didn't know the password, so I have no idea what's on it that might be of help in your investigation."

"Do you know anything else that might be of help?" Hoyt asked, signaling the interview was coming to an end.

Scott had not told him about Harold's cocaine use, or his silver travelling case. For all he knew, Hoyt already had the case in an evidence locker somewhere and was seeing if Scott would hide the information from him. He didn't care, he wasn't going to tell Hoyt anything that might reflect poorly on Harold. It was the detective's job to find out.

"No," said Scott. "I'm sorry. I was just along for the ride, and as Harold's assistant, professionally speaking."

"Do you own a gun?" asked Hoyt.

Scott was shocked. "A gun? No, I've never even held a gun. And how would I get one here on an airplane if I did?"

"You're right," said Hoyt. "I was just asking." Standing up, he said, "Thank you for your time, Mr. Harris, and I'm sorry for your loss."

Scott was glad to be done with the interview. He got up quickly, almost knocking his chair over. He extended his hand, shaking with Hoyt over the worst of circumstances.

"If you have any more questions ..." Scott offered.

"I know where to find you."

"Exactly."

"Please keep it that way," Hoyt said, as he led Scott out of the conference room.

Scott knew Hoyt was reminding him that he could not leave town. He'd been about to ask how long he was expected to stay in Lambertville. It would have been a mistake, making him appear less like a grieving widower and more like someone anxious to get away.

"Absolutely," Scott said, trying not to hurry as he walked down the hallway and out of the building.

CHAPTER 45

Hillsdale Estates is an over-fifty-five community located just off U.S. Route 202, equidistant between New Hope's largest grocery store and Peddler's Village, the sprawling complex of shops, restaurants and quaint landscaping that attracts a flood of locals and tourists in good weather. Among the smaller of its community type, the Estates, as people in the area call it, was built in the 1980s to accommodate an aging population. No children are allowed to live there, but plenty of them can be seen arriving to visit grandparents who'd purchased the homes and townhouses available.

Linda pulled onto Hillsdale Drive, the estate's main entrance, and drove a short distance until she saw Hamish Court. Turning right, she cruised along until she spotted a townhouse with the number 37 on it.

"They all look the same," Kyle said, peering through the car window as Linda parked on the street.

"Most of these places are like that," Linda replied. "Cookie cutter."

"Well, those are some big cookies. These are expensive homes. Danny and I looked at a few of them."

"Here?" Linda was surprised. Her friends had been in Lambertville less than a year.

"For fun," Kyle explained. "We're getting older, Linda. At some point we're going to think about ..."

"A place like this."

"Or not," Kyle said. "They're all over the country. We like Bethany Beach, too. Who knows?"

The four of them had gone to Bethany Beach, Delaware, for a week the previous summer. Linda wasn't a beach person, but she knew Kyle and Danny had taken a liking to the place and were attracted by the almost-nonexistent taxes in the state.

"But it won't be any time soon," said Kyle. "Now let's focus and see where this takes us."

The townhouse appeared, up close, to be a little worn. It looked like it hadn't been painted since construction, and the light lavender hue of the siding had faded. There was some cracking along the roof, but otherwise it was in good condition. The walkway was lined with daffodils and tulips, and four rose bushes grew beneath a large bay window. Kyle led them up to the door and rang the bell. A moment later a woman peeked out at him from the window. He waved at her, hoping the gesture made them seem harmless.

The door opened. A woman Kyle guessed to be in her seventies stood in the entrance. She was medium-height, with a plump, pleasant face, gray hair, and a red track outfit.

"May I help you?" she asked.

"We're looking for Polly Bryson," Kyle said. "Dean Robbins called her about us."

The woman had been smiling slightly; the smile faded at the mention of the call from Robbins.

"Who are you again?"

Kyle sensed her guard had gone up. He still didn't know if he was talking to Polly Bryson or not, since she had not acknowledged who she was.

"My name's Kyle Callahan. I run a bed and breakfast in Lambertville, and this is my friend, Linda Sikorsky."

"Pleased to meet you," Linda said.

The woman did not respond.

"You see," said Kyle, trying not to stammer, "we had two guests at our house who've been ... harmed in the past twenty-four hours."

"And you think I know something about it," the woman in the doorway said, confirming that she was Polly Bryson.

"Not about what happened to the men," Linda quickly said.

"That's right," Kyle added. "Not about that at all. But about their past. Well, Harold Summit's past, and Kevin Lockland's."

"Kevin was staying at your bed and breakfast?" said Bryson, startled.

"Oh, no, not at all. He was the nephew of Joseph Garland. Mr. Garland was staying at the house."

Bryson's face fell. "I saw that on the news, about the Garland man. It's terrible. Please, come in."

Polly Bryson stepped aside and welcomed them into her home. It was neat and tidy, with no clutter in sight. Kyle wondered if she had downsized when she'd moved here. A lot of older people made the effort to empty out their environments as age set in, partly to have less to care for, and partly so their loved ones didn't have to sort it all out when they were gone.

"I apologize for being standoffish," Polly said, ushering them into her living room. "You can't be too careful, especially with people disappearing or ending up dead. I'm not quite ready to make my exit yet. Would you like some coffee? It's already made."

We'd love some," Linda said, before Kyle had a chance to decline. She took a seat in one of two matching chairs angled to face each other in front of a faux fireplace. Several framed pictures were on the mantel, and Linda could see one was a wedding photograph with a young Polly Bryson and a man in an army uniform.

"I'll be right back," Polly said, leaving them as she headed into the kitchen. "I have some cookies, too. You can help me finish them off."

A moment later they were alone. Kyle took the opportunity to walk around the room, glancing at the immaculately dusted furniture. He walked over to the fireplace and looked at the photos.

"She was quite a looker," he said, peering at the wedding image. "And so was he."

"I don't see any children," Linda offered, indicating the half-dozen framed pictures.

"No," replied Kyle. "Friends and family, I'm guessing, but no children."

"That's correct," said Polly, coming in unheard behind them. She had a tray in her hands with three cups of coffee and a plate of cookies. A small silver creamer with matching sugar bowl and three spoons rested beside the cups. "Stuart and I never really wanted children. We talked about it because that's what young couples are supposed to do, but we never seriously considered it. I know it's uncommon, especially back then, but that's the way it was and I have no regrets."

Polly set the tray down on a coffee table and took a seat on the couch opposite Linda. Kyle sat in the second chair, and they began helping themselves to the coffee.

An awkward silence ensued, broken finally by Polly.

"So what do you want to know?" she asked. "It won't be

anything different from what I told Joseph Garland."

Kyle nearly dropped his cup.

"He was here?" he said, trying not to sound as surprised as he was. "Joseph Garland?"

"Assuming there was only one, yes," said Polly. "Yesterday afternoon."

Kyle thought quickly. Yesterday afternoon meant Garland had been to see her before, or possibly around the time, Harold Summit was murdered. By the following morning Garland, too, was dead. Six months earlier his nephew Kevin Lockland had vanished. Had something Polly Bryson told Joseph Garland gotten him killed? It was time to find out.

Kyle leaned forward, holding his coffee cup above his knees.

"Let's start from the beginning," Kyle said.

"And where would that be?" asked Polly.

"River Valley Bank," said Linda.

Polly Bryson sighed. "I was afraid of that," she said.

And they began to talk.

Polly didn't remember too much about her time with River Valley Bank, at least not the business of it. Money in, money out, she told them.

"After you've had a few million dollars pass through your hands—figuratively speaking—it all seems the same," she said.

The cookies were gone, and the coffee left in their cups had grown cold while Polly recalled her time as the branch manager.

"Accounts, ledgers, spreadsheets. I wasn't in it for that. And I was in banking for forty years! Not always with River Valley, that was my last stop. Dean tried to get me to move to Pennsylvania Trust with him and Harold, but I'd done my time in the corporate world." She glanced at the wedding photo on the mantel. "Joe passed in the winter twelve years ago, and I was ready to retire."

Gently prodding her to continue, Kyle said, "You were saying you weren't in it for the work, necessarily."

"Right, right. It was the people I liked. Banking is just a business, but it's a business that depends entirely on customers, especially when I started. Everything's online now, but back in those days there was a constant flow of people in and out of the bank. Local people. People I knew from across the street or who ran the shops in town. That's what made it rewarding."

Linda asked, "Do you remember anything specifically, anything that stood out involving Kevin and Harold? Did they work together much?"

"Well, Harold was Kevin's supervisor. Dean was my senior officer, and I was the branch manager. That was the pecking order, so to speak."

"Were you ever aware of an unhappy customer?"

Polly laughed. "Oh, all the time! They may live a block away from you, but money is money, you know what I mean? Especially with elderly clients. They misunderstand statements, they can't figure out where their money went ..."

Maybe into Kevin Lockland's offshore account, thought Kyle.

"What about loans?" he asked.

"What about them?"

"Were there customers who were particularly unhappy about being turned down, assuming you turned people down?"

"Of course!" Polly said. "At least once a week someone would come in ready to burn us to the ground. Some of them don't understand why they were denied, or they understand but don't accept that a bank is a business. We weren't a charity organization. Banks have overhead and regulations. It's all very scrutinized, which makes this whole embezzlement scandal at Pennsylvania Trust so odd—I don't believe for a minute that Kevin Lockland stole that money."

"And didn't leave a trace," Linda said.

"Because he didn't do it!" Polly sounded irritated at Linda's suggestion. "That's not who Kevin was. If he turned a loan down or had to repossess a house, he felt terrible about it, I know he did."

Kyle was struck by what she'd just said. "Repossess a house?" he asked.

"Oh, yes," Polly replied. "That was part of it all. Mortgages involve houses, Mr. Callahan."

Kyle felt foolish for sounding as if he hadn't known this. He and Danny had never had a mortgage, including for Passion House, but he knew most people who bought houses did it with loans from banks.

It got Kyle thinking on another track. "Was there anyone in particular who lost their house and was upset about it?"

Polly seemed to darken as she thought back to her days at the bank.

"Sometimes, yes," she said. "We had some threats, and one suicide I know of."

Kyle and Linda were silent a moment, then Kyle asked, "A suicide?"

"Very unfortunate. An elderly woman who lived on Wilson Street."

"Do you remember her name?" asked Linda.

"Nettles," Polly said. "Like the plant. I don't remember her first name. Is that terrible?"

"Not at all," Kyle said. "It's been a few years."

Polly smiled. "That's kind of you, 'a few years.' It goes so fast."

"Do you remember anything about that situation, with the Nettles woman?"

"No, not really," said Polly. "I'd have to see bank records, and of course that's not possible. I just remember Harold and Kevin being upset ... especially Kevin. He was younger and generous to a fault. But not a thief!"

"Of course not," said Linda.

"I think it's terrible, all the rumors about him. First with Harold, and then recently with the embezzlement."

Kyle was surprised. "What rumors involving Harold? Harold Summit?"

"That's the Harold you're here about, so yes," Polly said, perturbed. "There were rumors that Harold and Kevin had ... well, an affair, I suppose you'd call it."

What else would you call it? Kyle wondered.

"Harold was much older than Kevin," Kyle said, immediately thinking of Scott Harris, also many years his late husband's junior.

"He was," Polly said. "And nothing was ever proven, or confessed to. People like to gossip. It's another thing banks were famous for. Tellers are like hairs stylists and cashiers you've known for years. People feel comfortable telling them all sorts of things. But Harold and Kevin never admitted to an affair, and the whole thing just evaporated over time."

"Unless the affair heated up again," Linda said.

Polly looked shocked. "What did you say?"

"Nothing," Linda replied, quickly backtracking. "We're just

trying to find out what Joseph Garland may have discovered. We think it's at the heart of all this."

Polly took a breath and stood up. "Well, I wish you the best in finding out, assuming it doesn't end as poorly for you as it did for Mr. Garland."

The signal was clear. Kyle and Linda set their cups on the tray and got up.

"Thank you for taking the time," Kyle said.

Polly Bryson nodded and motioned toward the door. "I hope I was of some help."

She walked behind them as they prepared to leave the house. Kyle stopped by the door and looked at Polly.

"Did the Nettles woman have any family?" he asked.

Polly sighed. "I'm sorry, Mr. Callahan, I really don't know. I wasn't part of it. It was a tragedy that faded from people's minds, as most tragedies do. You'll have to keep searching for answers, I'm afraid."

"Oh," he said. "We will."

They headed down the walkway, watched by Polly Bryson until they'd gotten into the car. Fastening his seat belt, Kyle said, "I think I know someone who can help us."

"Who's that?" Linda asked, slipping her key into the ignition.

"Her name is Suzanne Cobb."

"From the Historical Group?"

Lambertville was old enough and large enough to have an organization devoted to its history, as well as the history of the surrounding towns and valley. Much of the area dated back to the earliest days of the United States and many people found that history fascinating. Suzanne Cobb was the main contact for the Lambertville Historical Group—she didn't have a title—and she'd been the person Kyle had turned to when he'd wanted to know the backstory of the house that became their bed and breakfast.

"You know her?" asked Kyle.

"She's been in the shop several times. Sure, I think everyone knows her. She's quite a colorful character."

"The perfect person to run a historical group," Kyle said. "You need the address?"

"I know where it is."

Just as Linda pulled away from the curb Kyle's phone rang. He took it out of its belt holster and glanced at the screen.

"That's odd."

"Who is it?" Linda said, answering her own question when she looked over and saw the name on Kyle's caller ID.

"Patty never calls," Kyle replied. "Something must have happened at the house." He clicked answer. "Patty, what's up?"

Kyle listened a moment, then said, "Why would Justin leave?"

Because he killed a man, Kyle thought as Patty spoke to him. *Possibly two.*

"We'll be there in fifteen minutes. No, don't call Sergeant Hoyt. Just wait for us."

He hung up and re-holstered his phone. "We have to go to Passion House. Patty's upset."

"About Justin?" Linda asked. "What about him?"

"She thinks he ran off, that he left town."

"But Hoyt told him to stay around. He told several people that."

"Exactly. And if Justin ignored him, it makes me wonder who else skipped out, too. Our evidence may be slipping away."

As Linda drove up the street, she said, "It's not our evidence, Kyle. It's Hoyt's evidence, very likely in multiple murders. "

"You're right, I'm sorry. I just get caught up."

"Like the old days."

Kyle nodded silently. He didn't want to admit to himself that he'd been sucked back into a very dangerous game, a game that had almost cost him his life.

"He's just scared," Kyle said. "I can't imagine Justin would kill anyone, and for what? I'm sure he got what he wanted from men in other ways. He has the looks, if not the smarts."

"Maybe Patty thinks the same thing and she's worried he'll get in trouble."

"Well, he will!" Kyle said. "You don't flee a crime scene, and that's what it looks like he's doing. But let's not jump to conclusions. We'll hear Patty out, why she even thinks he's gone, and take it from there."

"And then we go see Suzanne Cobb."

A few minutes later they'd crossed back over the bridge into Lambertville and were pulling into the driveway at Passion House. Patty was waiting on the porch.

CHAPTER 46

Gladys felt more trapped by the hour. Hoyt had made it clear that their interviews at the police station were not the last he expected to see of them.

"How long are we supposed to stay here?" she asked Carol as she paced their suite. The more she looked at the mural of the Manhattan skyline, the more she longed to be there instead. She'd disliked New York, but she would never hate it, or anywhere else, as much as she hated Lambertville at that moment.

"He didn't say," replied Carol. She'd been sitting at the small desk provided as part of the room's decor.

"Until they arrest someone?" Gladys continued. "What if that's a week from now, a month? Are the police going to pay for our room? I don't want to be here anymore, Carol. Let's please pack and go."

Carol didn't respond. She'd been looking at her phone more frequently over the past hour, as if something of great importance had happened in the world and she had to stay updated on the latest reports.

"What are you looking at?" Gladys asked, annoyed. "You've been glued to that thing. You know I hate it when people pay more attention to their phones than they do to each other."

Gladys had a flip phone. She'd refused to get anything more advanced, and she hated calling handheld devices "smart." Smartphones, smart-this, smart-that. The only thing she considered smart were people, and not many of those.

"Nothing," Carol replied, as she turned her phone over and slid it away from her.

Gladys caught the movement and marched over to the desk.

"You're hiding something."

"I'm not," Carol protested. "I just ..."

Gladys took the phone and looked at it. She began reading what she saw on screen, her face falling with each sentence.

"What is this?" Gladys asked.

"It's nothing," Carol replied. "Gossip, really. Nothing for you to be concerned with."

The more Gladys read what she'd found on Carol's phone, the more agitated she became.

"They're saying I had something to do with it."

"They're not saying you killed him," Carol clarified.

"No, just that I had him killed. That's insane!"

Gladys put the phone down and began pacing again.

"I couldn't have killed him. He was murdered on a trail, or a canal or something. I don't hike! I barely even walk. Where is this coming from?"

Gladys waited, watching Carol as she carefully chose her words.

"You can be abrasive sometimes," Carol said.

"You mean a bitch?"

"I wouldn't put it that way."

"And so what if I am? Does that mean I'd hire someone to kill Harold Summit?"

"Of course not, Sweetheart. It's just ... blood in the water, you see? People predisposed to not liking you sense an opportunity."

"To shove a knife in."

"Well, yes."

"To hammer a nail in my coffin."

"Given the chance."

"And me exposing Summit in a room full of writers was the chance they'd been waiting for."

"Exactly."

Gladys was fuming. She walked to the window and peered down.

"Let them talk," she said, staring at the street below. "Let them indulge in the small poisons of small minds. In the meantime, find out when the hell we can leave! We're not under arrest. They can't just keep us here, can they?"

"I'll see what I can learn," Carol replied. "Maybe we can go home and teleconference or something if they need us."

"Maybe," Gladys replied, distracted by something she saw outside. "They're back," she continued a moment later. "The Callahan fellow and that tall blonde. She's quite something."

Gladys kept staring down at the street as Kyle and Linda arrived at the house. She did not see Patty on the porch below, or Carol's stricken face at the mention of the attractive Linda Sikorsky. Gladys had never hesitated to express her appreciation for a good looking woman. That's as far as it had ever gone, and she saw no harm in it.

"I'll find out how long we have to stay here," Carol said.

"You do that," replied Gladys. "And don't let Hoyt be evasive. Tell him if he wants us here indefinitely he'll have to pay for the room and meals. Remind him I'm just a writer nobody reads. The rich writer is dead."

"I don't think I have to remind him of that."

"No," said Gladys, finally turning away from the window. "I don't suppose you do."

CHAPTER 47

Being seen as little more than an appendage to Harold Summit hadn't bothered Scott before—or so he'd told himself—but now that Harold was dead and the story had taken on national significance, his invisibility and irrelevance were almost more than he could bear. He knew he should have expected this, but then, he'd never expected Harold to die, and certainly not at the hands of a killer. He'd fantasized Harold's passing away in another ten or fifteen years, possibly secreted at the end of his life in a posh nursing home where Scott would be his caretaker and guardian, offering "no comment" to anyone doing stories on the once-famous author. It would be costly, but by then they would have transferred Harold's assets into Scott's name so Medicaid would pick up the bill, and Scott would be living nicely but modestly in a house in Palm Springs. That had been the plan, an image of his future he had never shared with Harold.

But now? Now he was a widower no one knew about. An assistant whose marriage to Harold had been performed at the Los Angeles County Clerk's office, taking up an hour of their time before Harold hurried off to meet his book agent. His agent didn't know he'd just gotten married. Nobody knew except two of Harold's friends who'd gone with them, one to serve as a witness. It had been just another day, and it should have been a warning: you will always be in the background, Scott Harris. You will not be thanked in any books, introduced at any events, or walked down any red carpets on the arm of your husband.

Scott had been getting phone calls from Harold's friends who had his number, but he'd let them to go voicemail. He didn't like most of them, anyway. Harold was the sort of man who attracted people like himself who were tolerable only if you loved them. What bothered Scott was that no one from the press had attempted to contact him. Surely, he thought, they must know he exists. It's part of a reporter's job. While his marriage to Harold had been low-key and seldom discussed, it wasn't unknown. It wasn't as if Scott was some family secret kept locked in an attic. So why had no one come to Passion House, or called and asked to speak to the husband of the victim?

Because they don't know about you, thought Scott, *and they don't care.* Harold hadn't wanted them to care. He hadn't wanted one tiny speck of the spotlight shining on anyone but Harold Summit.

In a way he was grateful. He knew it was only a matter of time before details of the investigation made their way into news stories. The police would find Harold's little silver case and the cocaine inside. They would retrace Harold's last movements and discover ... what? That he'd tricked with someone in the bushes, someone who'd killed him for his watch or the cash in his wallet? Whatever the police knew the press would soon know, too, and then it would all come out. Scott's anonymity was a blessing of sorts. It gave him time, something he needed to sort things out and make whatever arrangements he could before leaving Lambertville forever. Whatever happened, it was not a place he would return to. And he had options now, he could move wherever he wanted to live. It would not be Los Angeles. He hated the place. Palm Springs, despite being part of his fantasy for their later years, was too hot. Scott liked the northeast and could see himself living in a nice condo in Philadelphia, or maybe even Chicago. But first he had to have money, and that was proving to be a challenge.

Harold maintained life insurance for both of them. He'd considered it prudent, and while it was only a quarter million dollars, it was something. Combined with Harold's estate, it would leave Scott in a very good position. The problem now was that the insurance company had balked when Scott called them. They couldn't pay out, they said, until an investigation had been completed.

"He's dead," Scott had said to the woman he'd managed to reach after pressing several numbers that bounced him around until he finally got a human on the line. "What more do you need to know?"

She'd put him on hold, talked to someone above her pay grade, then had come back on and told him it was company policy to wait for the results of the police investigation, as well as conducting one of their own if needed.

"You mean to determine if I killed him," Scott said.

The woman had not replied.

"You don't pay beneficiaries if they killed the person with the policy," Scott said. "I can understand that. But I didn't kill my husband, just so you know."

"I'm not suggesting that."

"Yes, you are," Scott said, and hung up.

That had been an hour ago, and now he was standing by the window of the Margaret Suite looking down as Kyle and Linda arrived. He watched them get out of the car and head into the house. He hoped that soon he would never have to see them again.

CHAPTER 48

Kyle could see Patty on the porch as they drove up to the house and Linda parked by the curb.

"She's been waiting," Linda said, turning the car off.

They got out and hurried along the walkway. They still needed to see Suzanne Cobb at the Historical Group and time was quickly passing.

"Patty, what's going on?" Kyle asked when they reached the top of the steps.

"He's left town, Mr. Callahan, I know he has."

"Come into the house and tell me."

Kyle opened the front door and led them all into the parlor. "Sit, please," he said to Patty, as he took a seat himself in one of the chairs.

Linda and Patty sat on the couch, Linda easing into it while Patty perched nervously on the edge of the cushion.

"What makes you think Justin left Lambertville?" Linda asked.

"I know for a fact he did," Patty replied.

"And how do you know this?" Kyle asked.

Patty took a moment to gather herself. She looked nervously at Linda, then cast her eyes quickly down and said, "I have a friend in town. She told me."

Kyle and Linda exchanged glances. Patty had a woman friend? A woman *like Linda*?

Kyle hoped his surprise and fascination didn't show on his face. Being lesbian had not been among Patty's mysteries before that moment. He and Danny had never suspected it.

"And what did your friend tell you?" Linda asked, attempting to keep the conversation moving.

"She told me she saw Justin getting on the bus."

"The Trans-Bridge bus?" Kyle asked. He assumed that was the one, since there weren't any other commuter buses that stopped nearby.

"Yes."

"But which way was the bus going? To New York or to

Doylestown?"

If Justin had gone to Doylestown he hadn't gone far, Kyle thought.

"To New York City," replied Patty. "She knows about the murder of Mr. Summit, and what happened to Mr. Garland."

I'm sure she knows a lot of things, Kyle thought. *Pillow talk, Patty?* He couldn't keep himself from smiling at the thought.

The smile caught Linda's eye and she looked at him disapprovingly. The smile disappeared.

"She called me and told me our houseboy—that's what she calls Justin—had gotten on the bus, and off he went."

No "Mr. Stritch" for Justin, Kyle thought, noticing Patty had used Justin's first name. *Maybe she considers him below her rank, or beneath her.*

"There's more," Patty said. "After Marlene called me—"

Marlene, thought Kyle. *This is the most she's told us about her life since we hired her.*

"—I tried to reach Justin. I dialed his cell phone several times."

Linda: "And he didn't answer."

"That's correct. It went to voicemail. I wasn't sure if I should call you or Sergeant Hoyt."

Kyle didn't want Hoyt involved again until he and Linda had something solid to tell the detective. They were close to the truth, he was sure of it, and informing Hoyt that Justin had left town could distract them from finding the killer. Kyle seriously doubted Justin had murdered Harold Summit, or that he'd had anything to do with Joseph Garland's death. Justin wasn't much more than a kid, at least emotionally, and Kyle didn't think he would do anything more serious than break an older man's heart now and then.

"You didn't call Hoyt, did you?" Kyle asked.

"No, Mr. Callahan, I did not. Would you like me to?"

"Not at all, Patty. In fact, Linda and I were on our way to see someone. We think we'll have information for Sergeant Hoyt soon, and I'd rather wait to speak to him when we do ... if you don't mind."

"Not at all," Patty said, standing up. She appeared relieved to be done talking to them. She smoothed the folds her of skirt and said, "I'm not one to get involved in things that aren't my business, but Justin works here, and Mr. Summit and Mr. Garland were our guests."

"That makes it your business, Patty," Kyle assured her. "You did the right thing."

Patty was about to leave when Kyle said, "By the way, have you ever heard the name Nettles?"

Patty stopped and looked at him. Thinking about it, she said, "No, I haven't. Is that a place?"

"It's the last name of someone," Kyle replied. "I don't have a first name."

"Is it a name I should know?"

"Apparently not," said Kyle. "There was an incident with River Valley Bank some years ago, and one of their customers committed suicide."

Shock showed on Patty's face. "Oh, my."

"We think it's connected to all this," Kyle said. "We were told it was a tragedy in the community and I thought you might know about it."

"When did this happen?"

"About fifteen years ago," Linda said. "Harold Summit worked at the bank then, along with Mr. Garland's nephew."

"I see," said Patty. "There may be a connection, then. But I wasn't living in Lambertville fifteen years ago."

"No?" asked Kyle.

"No, Mr. Callahan. I was living in Philadelphia, working as a live-in housekeeper and nanny of sorts. I can give you the family's name if you'd like to contact them, in case you want to verify that."

"I'm not looking for an alibi," Kyle said, laughing. "I just thought you might have heard about this Nettles business."

"I'm afraid not," Patty said. "But I'll ask my friend. She may know something."

Patty was about to leave the room when Kyle said, "We'd love to meet her sometime. You should feel free to invite her over."

Patty blushed and looked at the floor. She nodded, committing nothing to words.

Just as Patty was about to exit Kyle looked across the room and saw Scott Harris standing on the staircase. Kyle stared at him a moment, wondering how long he'd been there and what he'd heard.

Patty saw him, too, and hurried into the kitchen.

"Mr. Harris," Kyle said, as Linda got up from the couch. "Are you holding up okay?"

Scott made no move to continue down the stairs. "As well as a man whose husband was just murdered could be doing, I suppose."

Kyle had no response to that. Instead, he said, "I was wondering if we could get a few minutes of your time."

"We?"

"Linda and myself. There are just a few things we'd like to sort out, and you may be able to help us."

Scott frowned at them, thought about it, and said, "Of course. Although I've told the sergeant everything I know, and I'm a little on the talked-out side."

"That's fine," said Kyle. "We won't take much of your time."

"Come along, then," Scott said.

He turned and headed back up the stairs, with Kyle and Linda following behind.

CHAPTER 49

Kyle was struck by how much of the Margaret Suite he hadn't paid attention to the last few months. He and Danny had been so occupied by the business side of running the house that he'd forgotten some of the finer details. Having named it after Danny's beloved boss and mentor, they had taken pains to make it look and feel as much like her apartment above the restaurant as possible in a single large room with an en suite bathroom. There were even photographs from Margaret's home placed around the room, including one of her and her husband Gerard from their early days in New York City. Guests were free to imagine for themselves who the people in the pictures were.

Kyle had taken one of the overstuffed chairs, with Linda sitting in the other and Scott perched stiffly on the edge of the bed.

"What did you want to ask me?" Scott said. He kept glancing toward the window. It made Kyle think of a bird, or a cat, who wanted out of the enclosed space it had found itself in.

"A few things," said Kyle.

"Shoot," said Scott. Then he winced. "Maybe not the right word."

Kyle took a breath, weighing his words.

"Did Harold talk much about his life before you met? And when *did* you meet, exactly?"

"We met five years ago when I was working at the deli, at the Giant in New Hope. I'd never seen him before and didn't know he'd once lived in Lambertville until we had dinner that night."

"So you wouldn't know about his life before he was a writer," said Linda.

"Although he must had talked about it, yes?" added Kyle. "You were married, I assume he talked about his life before ..."

"The fame and fortune?" asked Scott.

"Well, yes."

Scott smiled wearily. "The answer is no, he did not. Harold was a very private man, even with me. Maybe especially with me. I always had the feeling he didn't want there to be a Harold Summit before the bestseller lists. It was odd and a little sad,

170

considering his success didn't come until later in life. But once it came he made the most of it."

"So he enjoyed being famous," Linda said.

"Who wouldn't? He also enjoyed talking about it," Scott replied. "If you didn't know he was somebody, you at least knew he was rich."

Linda and Kyle looked at each other, an exchange Scott noticed.

"That makes me wealthy now, doesn't it?" said Scott. "At least that's what you're thinking. You and the police. But I'm used to people assuming I was with Harold for the money. I can't say it doesn't bother me, but it sure as hell doesn't make me a murderer. Why are you asking about his previous life, anyway?"

"Not all of it," Kyle clarified. "We're looking at a specific timeframe, when he worked at River Valley Bank."

Scott looked confused and surprised. "Harold worked at a *bank*? When was this?"

"Fifteen years ago," Linda said. "At least that's when it ended, sometime around then. He worked at the bank for a number of years before that."

Scott looked momentarily stunned. "I can't believe he never told me that. I thought ..."

"That he'd always been a writer?" asked Kyle.

"Well, yeah," said Scott. "He didn't talk like he'd ever done anything else. But now that you're telling me this, I feel really foolish. Of course he hadn't been a writer all those years, but I didn't ask, and he didn't tell. Just like he never told me he'd been the editor for some small literary magazine. That's how Gladys Finch claims to know him — and accuse him. But Harold and I had a good life. He talked about what he chose to talk about, and that was it. He wasn't a man to reveal anything he didn't want you to know."

"So nothing about prior relationships?" Kyle said, thinking about the rumors of an affair with Kevin Lockland.

"Nothing," Scott replied.

Kyle sensed hesitation. "But?"

"Hookups," Scott said. "One-offs. *Tricks.* Harold liked what we used to call anonymous sex, and if you ask me, that's where the police should be looking. They still haven't found his phone. Maybe it was some young guy who thought he could get a couple hundred dollars for it."

Kyle was disappointed by the conversation. It hadn't told them more than they'd already known. Scott Harris had shockingly insufficient knowledges of his late husband's life before they'd met, but Kyle knew they had both probably wanted it that way.

"How did you decide to stay at Passion House?" Linda asked.

Kyle was struck by the question. It wasn't one he'd considered.

"Yes," he said, "how did you and Harold know about this place?"

"A fan on Facebook," said Scott.

"One of your friends?" asked Linda.

"Oh, no, not at all. Harold had a fan page ... a business page."

Kyle knew perfectly well what Scott was talking about. Passion House had its own page, with Kyle as the administrator. He and Danny both had Facebook profiles, but Danny had not spent more than ten minutes on his in all the years he'd had it. He considered Facebook a reflection of modern society's ills and had no use for it other than as a tool to promote businesses.

"Harold rarely posted anything," Scott continued. "I was the one doing it all. I used his account so people would think it was him, but he never had any real interest in it."

"And who was the fan who recommended us?" Kyle asked.

"One of six thousand seventy-two. I don't know who it was, not in real life, but once I posted about coming to the mystery writers conference, this person kept saying Passion House was the best place in town and we really must stay here."

Kyle sensed something unusual about this. They'd only been open to the public for a few months. Their own Facebook page had just over a hundred followers. What were the odds of one of Harold Summit's fans knowing about the place and insisting they stay here?

"Does the person have a name?" Linda asked.

"Just an initial and a last name," Scott said. "T. Barnabus."

Kyle thought about it. "Tom? Todd? Timothy?"

"It could be anyone," Linda said. "Facebook is riddled with fake and anonymous accounts. They don't ask to see your birth certificate."

"True," said Kyle.

Scott stood up from the bed. "I'm sorry I couldn't be more helpful. *Really*. The last thing I want is for anyone to keep thinking I had something to do with this."

"You were more than helpful," Kyle said, knowing it wasn't true. "And we're so sorry you're going through this. Thank you for taking the time to talk with us."

Kyle and Linda were about to leave the suite.

"There is one thing," Scott said. "Harold had gotten some emails a few weeks before the trip. Threatening kind of emails."

This piqued Kyle's interest. "What were they about?"

"I can't say, exactly. Harold didn't show them to me. He just said he'd gotten several emails through his website contact page about justice being patient, crimes catching up to you, he wasn't that clear about it."

"But he took them seriously?" asked Linda.

"Yes and no. He took them seriously enough to tell me about them, but not enough to save them! When I asked to read them, he told me he'd deleted them. They were rubbish, he said. Just another nutcase that any successful author had to deal with."

"But you're not convinced he thought that."

"Not now," said Scott. "Now I think it was a warning."

"Did you tell Sergeant Hoyt about the emails?" Kyle asked.

"I'd forgotten them until you got me talking about Facebook and the trip here. I'll give him a call if you think it's important."

"I think it could be very important," said Kyle. "And thank you again for your time. We'll leave you alone now."

Scott stayed by the bed and watched as Kyle and Linda headed downstairs. It was time for a trip to the Historical Group and another look into Harold Summit's past.

CHAPTER 50

The Lambertville Historical Group is located in a small office on Bridge Street two doors down from the River Brew Coffee Shop. It shares the space with Victor Lehman, CPA, an accounting firm consisting of Victor and his daughter, Rita Parker.

The Historical Group was founded in the 1970s during a time when Lambertville was on the decline and its history was in danger of fading away. The first president of the Group, a man named George Weather, wanted to preserve the town's past. An eccentric visionary, George had predicted that someday Lambertville would thrive again, although he had not anticipated its revival as a liberal enclave. He'd imagined industry returning to the town, with trains continuing to bring commuters and tourists from the big cities. The trains were long gone now, and the only industry in town was a microbrewery and the Dahl House Jams factory, along with local artisans. But George Weather had been right, and Lambertville had become one of the most vibrant, prized communities in the Delaware Valley.

Kyle first became aware of the Historical Group when he and Danny were considering buying the property that became Passion House. He'd wanted to know about the mansion's history—and judging from its size, it would have been considered a mansion at the time it was built. That's how he learned about the house's builder, Noah Habermeier, and the saga of the Habermeier family. He also learned a great deal about Lambertville and the surrounding area, most of it from the current president of the Group, Suzanne Cobb.

Kyle found the Historical Group when he'd done a search of the town online. He and Danny were still in New York City at the time, and after discovering there was a group devoted to the history of Lambertville, he reached out with an email and ended up engaging in a lively correspondence with Suzanne. To Kyle's surprise and dismay, Suzanne was a fan of murder mysteries. It didn't take long for her to do some sleuthing of her own and discover things about Kyle that he'd rather she not know— specifically his close relationship to several murderers and how he'd stopped them from continuing their killing sprees. For Kyle and Danny, Lambertville was about moving on, entering a new phase in their lives, and Suzanne had made that more complicated than he'd wanted it to be. But after her her initial prying (he told he'd seen a therapist about it all and preferred to leave those events behind him), she became a reliable friend. She helped them get used to their life in a new town. He suspected she would be more than happy to talk about the recent deaths of Harold Summit and Joseph Garland, and if they might be connected to a local tragedy from years ago.

"If anyone knows about this Nettles incident, it's Suzanne," Kyle said as they drove over to the Historical Group. They'd switched cars at the house and Kyle was driving.

"According to Polly Bryson it was common knowledge, kind of a big deal in town."

"But not big enough for her to remember the woman's first name."

"I suppose I could do an online search," replied Kyle. "There might be something there."

"We're about to ask Suzanne Cobb, you might as well wait."

Linda was right. They were a block from the Group's office, there was no point in doing an online search, and no time. Kyle had called ahead to make sure Suzanne would be there and she was expecting them. He hadn't told her why they were coming, only that he had some questions about events from fifteen years ago. He knew that would pique her interest, and she'd told him she would be there waiting.

Kyle parked the car and paid for an hour on the meter. They wouldn't need nearly that long, but it would give them time for coffee at the River Brew if they wanted to toss around ideas after learning whatever Suzanne had to tell them.

Suzanne Cobb looked familiar to Linda, and she said so when they walked into the small office.

"You've been in my store," Linda said, recognizing Suzanne as a customer whose name she'd never known. "I'm Linda Sikorsky. I own *For Pete's Sake* in New Hope."

"I love that place!" Suzanne said, ignoring Linda's extended hand to give her a hug instead.

Suzanne was short and plump, and she reminded Kyle of the late actress Shirley Booth, whose TV show *Hazel* was a hit when he was a kid. She even sounded like Shirley Booth. Thinking about it as he watched Suzanne throw her arms around Linda, he realized how old it made him feel. He wondered if anyone younger than fifty remembered the actress.

"And Kyle, how nice to see you!" Suzanne exclaimed, moving quickly to give Kyle an equally enthusiastic hug. "Come, sit, I understand you have some questions and I'm dying to hear them."

Here we go, thought Kyle. *She knows about Summit's murder and she thinks that's why we're here. An astute woman.*

Suzanne led them into the main office area, where a coffee table, two chairs and a chaise welcomed visitors, along with a small desk that looked like it got little use. Linda and Kyle each took a chair, while Suzanne settled onto the chaise.

"Now what can I help you with? Does this have anything to do with that poor Harold Summit's death? And I understand there was another one in Stockton."

"Yes," said Kyle. "Joseph Garland. Although the police haven't yet announced a cause of death with him."

"But you suspect they're connected."

She sounded a little too excited by the prospect of murder in their small community, but he needed her knowledge of Lambertville's history and notable events.

"We're actually here about something that took place a while ago," Linda said.

Suzanne's disappointment showed. "Oh, really? So it's not about what's happened with these gentlemen, which is awful enough, of course."

"Of course," said Kyle. "It may be connected, but we don't know. That's what we're trying to find out."

"And what is it?"

"A suicide," Linda said.

That appeared to cheer her up. Suicide was another form of murder, after all, and often more mysterious than your typical crime of passion.

"Who are you talking about?" asked Suzanne.

"Someone named Nettles," Kyle answered. "A woman, but we don't know her first name. We just know it involved a problem with the old River Valley Bank. Apparently she was denied a loan or a mortgage, and she killed herself."

Suzanne sat thinking for several moments, then it came to her. "I remember that!" she said. "Her name was Louise Nettles. I remember it quite well, now that you've brought it up. It was very sad. She jumped off the bridge in Stockton."

The bridge in Stockton, thought Kyle. *The same bridge Joseph Garland's body was found floating near. Had he gone there looking for a final piece of the puzzle? Or had he been lured there to be killed in the same spot where Louise Nettles had ended her life?*

"Tell us what you know," Linda said, as she and Kyle gave Suzanne Cobb their undivided attention.

CHAPTER 51

"They can't keep us here," Gladys said, folding a pair of jeans and putting them into her suitcase. She had started packing, something she normally left up to Carol, an hour after they'd returned from the police station.

"I don't know what the rules are," Carol said, standing by the window and watching Gladys. It was a sight seldom seen and somewhat fearsome: a caged Gladys Finch restless to take action, and that's exactly how Gladys had described herself after nearly wearing a path in the rug. "I feel like I'm being confined here," Gladys had said, as she reached her breaking point. Then she pulled her suitcase out of the closet and started filling it.

"The rules are what we say they are," Gladys said. "Unless they arrest me, they can't just tell me to stay here. It doesn't work that way."

"How would you know how it works?"

"I don't watch television, that's how. All these ideas people have about forensics and police procedures and all that, they get them from television ... most people anyway. They think you can get DNA test results before the next commercial break, and that when some small town cop tells you to stick around, why, of course you have to! Well, Carol, we don't have to, and we're not going to. Now please pack."

Carol reluctantly got the second suitcase out of the closet and slowly started putting her clothes in it, first one item, then another, piece by piece.

Watching her, Gladys said, "What are you waiting for? The police to call and say they've made an arrest? We're leaving, Carol, *now*."

"What if they want us to testify or something?"

"In a trial?"

"Yes, Honeybunch."

Gladys rolled her eyes at that.

"Then they can contact us and ask us to come back, although we have nothing to testify to."

"You threatened a murder victim," Carol said. "A jury may

want to know why, and what you said."

"I said he was a thief," Glady snapped. "I never said he deserved to be killed for it. Now please, just pack. I want to be gone before anyone else gets back."

Carol knew that by "anyone else" Gladys meant the owners of the bed and breakfast. They had no way of knowing Danny was in the guest house, only that Kyle had left with the Sikorsky woman. They'd seen them drive away.

"We have to pay for the entire stay," Carol said, as if Gladys intended to skip out on their bill.

"I know that! I'm not trying to get out of paying. *I'm trying to get out of Lambertville!* Now please, hurry up."

Carol picked up her pace, taking clothes from the dresser and folding them into the suitcase.

Gladys had finished with hers and was zipping it up when she stopped, cocked her head and listened. Carol saw her and looked at her curiously.

"Do you hear that?" Gladys asked.

"What, Honeybear?"

Gladys glared at her. "Make up your mind, Carol. Is it Honeybunch or Honeybear? Or better yet, neither. I know you like these terms of endearment, but they grate."

Carol blushed a deep red.

"There it is," Gladys said.

Carol heard it too, now. "It's a phone, *Gladys*."

"Well, someone needs to answer it. That's the most annoying ringtone I've ever heard."

Gladys finished zipping up her suitcase and yanked it off the bed. "Hurry, this place gives me the creeps. I don't want to be the third person staying here they find dead."

Carol was still burning from being called out over the nicknames. She knew Gladys was just in a mood—she was often in a mood—and that it would pass. The best thing she could do now was finish packing as quickly as possible and get them out of there.

CHAPTER 52

Scott heard the women talking across the hall. He knew from his brief encounters with Gladys Finch that she could be prickly, but it sounded as if they were arguing about something.

He could understand it if they were, given the stresses they were all under since Harold's murder. Joseph Garland's mysterious death had only magnified the tensions, and Scott assumed it wouldn't be long before an enterprising reporter showed up at Passion House asking how it was that two guests were found dead within a day of each other. The chances of its being a coincidence were slim, but Scott didn't want to be around long enough to find out what the deaths had in common.

He had hoped Sergeant Hoyt could give him a timeline, specifically a limit on how long he had to stay in Lambertville. He would have to be there to claim Harold's body, obviously, and to participate as required in any police investigation. But he hoped to be out of town within a few days, and he expected never to see the area again. It didn't matter to him that he'd spent most of his life here, or that he'd met Harold here. Harold had been murdered a mile from where Scott was standing looking out the window, and he wanted to leave with no plans of ever returning.

He'd tried a dozen times to call Harold. He knew someone had turned the phone off—most likely the someone who'd put a bullet into Harold and left him in the canal. Still, the gesture was a habit, and habits were often stronger than reason. He walked to the dresser, picked up his phone, and dialed Harold's number one more time. *Please, please, someone pick up. Tell me you found his phone on the towpath, or in a trash can, anywhere.*

He heard it then, the distinctive ringtone Harold had liked so much: the opening theme from the old Batman television series. Harold had confessed to having a crush on Adam West when he was a teenager. For a moment Scott wasn't sure if he was imagining it. He stopped and listened. The women across the hall apparently heard it too, as their voices went silent while the phone rang twice, three times ... and finally stopped.

He's back! Scott thought, knowing it was irrational and

impossible. Harold was dead. But his phone, or at least one with the very same ringtone, was somewhere in the house.

Scott walked out into the hallway. He looked downstairs, then toward the staircase leading up to the third floor. Where had the ringtone come from? The only way to find out was to dial again, so he did.

And there it was, ringing noisily, sending its Bat-Signal out for everyone to hear. The sound was more muffled this time, as if someone had covered it up, but he heard it clearly. He looked toward the staircase and knew the sound was coming from upstairs, where the staff lived.

He walked slowly but deliberately to the landing.

"Harold?" he called up. "Who's up there? That's my husband's phone!"

He began climbing the stairs, his gut clenching with a mixture of fear, apprehension and excitement. Whoever was up there had Harold's phone, and was most assuredly responsible for his death. Scott thought about calling the police but gave in to his curiosity instead. The ringing stopped then, but Scott kept going.

CHAPTER 53

"I didn't know Louise Nettles personally," Suzanne said. "Few people did. She was reclusive."

Suzanne had needed a few moments to gather her thoughts. She stared out the office window, as if peering into her memory, then began recalling incidents as she remembered them.

"She had a house on Wilson Street, as I recall. It wasn't well-kept, which is why I remember it ... why most people remembered it. She was a bit of a hoarder."

"You'd been inside her house?" asked Linda, surprised.

"Oh, no! This was outside, in her back yard and along a fence."

"What kinds of things did she hoard?" Kyle asked.

"I really should choose my words better," Suzanne said. "She wasn't a hoarder like you see on TV, she just had old appliances and things like that lying around. I think she resold the stuff and she probably didn't have anywhere else to put it."

Wanting to get to the point of their visit, Kyle said, "What happened at the bank?"

"Why did she kill herself?" added Linda.

Suzanne looked at them curiously. "We never really know that, do we? Why someone kills themself. But with Louise, we heard about the bank situation because it was such a sad story."

"And what was the story?" asked Kyle, feeling impatient.

"The bank took her house," Suzanne explained. "Or they were about to. I don't really know the details, not well enough to tell you who was involved or who made what decision."

Harold Summit, thought Kyle. *Kevin Lockland. Were there others, dead or alive?*

"She was about to be evicted," Suzanne finished.

"By the bank?" asked Linda.

"By the police, in service to the bank. I can't tell you what transpired, I wasn't there, but before they could physically come and force her out of her home, she jumped off the bridge."

"That's so sad," Kyle said.

"What made it even sadder was that she'd been so alone. By

182

choice, I think, but it still made for quite the story around town."

Kyle thought about it all, then said, "So she had no family? No one who could have helped her?"

"As I said earlier, I didn't know her to speak of, but after her death I learned she did have two children, they just didn't live here ... hadn't lived here for some time."

"Did you ever know their names?"

"I'm trying to think," Suzanne said, searching her memory. "She had a son and a daughter, I remember that. The son left Lambertville years before, so he couldn't have been much more than a kid when he took off, and the daughter ..."

"She moved away, too?" asked Linda.

"Yes, but who knows why? And if there'd ever been a husband in the picture, I never heard about it." Then, with a flash of recollection, she blurted, "Leland and Patricia! Those were their names."

Kyle and Linda listened, taking a moment to make the connection.

"The son, Leland, I don't think he ever returned. It was the daughter who came back and buried her mother. She made quite a scene at the bank, but there was nothing they could have done. Banks are not charities, and not many adult children can pay off a parent's house. It's mostly hearsay, you understand. I just remember people talking about it."

"Of course," said Kyle, wondering if Suzanne Cobb could see his hands visibly trembling as recognition dawned on him.

"One person tells someone, and that person tells someone else. That's how I know most of this story."

Kyle could tell by the look on Linda's face that she, too, knew the significance of the name.

"Did she stay in town?" Linda asked. "The daughter, Patricia?"

"I can't say!" Suzanne replied. "I never saw her. I wasn't involved in any of this. I hope that's not what you thought coming to see me."

"Not at all," Kyle reassured her. "We just thought you may have seen this Patricia around that time, and possibly since."

"The answer to both is no, obviously. If I'd seen her then I would know what she looked like, but I didn't, Kyle. Why, is this someone you know?"

"I'm not sure," replied Kyle. "I can't be certain at this point. There are plenty of women named Patricia."

"Maybe she goes by Tricia," Louise offered.

"Or Patty," said Linda.

"Yes," replied Kyle, as he quickly stood up from the chair.

The move surprised Suzanne. Linda stood up, too, as she and Kyle made clear they were about to leave.

"So soon?" asked Suzanne, quickly getting up. "Is everything all right?"

"You've been very helpful," Kyle said, taking her hand. "We need to get back to Passion House."

As Suzanne walked them to the door, she said, "I've told everyone they must stay there when they visit. My out of town friends, obviously. There's no reason for anyone in Lambertville to stay there, that would be silly!"

As she held the door for them, Suzanne added, "Say hello to Danny for me. And remember to think about the tour."

The Historical Group wanted to add Passion House to the list of homes it displayed on their annual Historical Homes tour. The house had been locked up for years before Kyle and Danny bought it, and Suzanne wanted to share the home's past with tour goers.

"That's a yes," Kyle said. "We just need time to plan it. We'll talk soon."

"Soon!" said Suzanne, waving as they walked quickly to the car.

Closing the car door and reaching for her seatbelt, Linda said, "What now? Do you really think it's her?"

"I do," replied Kyle, starting the car. "And I think she's on a mission. I'll drive, you call Sergeant Hoyt. Ask him to meet us at Passion House. I hope we're wrong. I hope this is all a terrible coincidence, but if Patty Langley is Patricia Nettles, she's armed and dangerous."

Kyle sped away from the curb as Linda took out her cell phone and dialed.

CHAPTER 54

Patty had just placed the phone in Justin's nightstand when it began ringing. The sound was odd and startling. She recognized the ringtone from somewhere, which is what made her hesitate while it continued ringing. It was so unexpected, so shocking at that moment, that she just stood there staring into the drawer at the phone she'd taken from a dead Harold Summit. And then it stopped.

She closed the drawer and was about to hurry out of the room when it rang again. She froze halfway to the doorway, turned back and looked at the nightstand. She wondered if she should shut the phone off. But that would defeat the purpose of putting it there. She could mute it, but that might seem deliberate to the police. Did people really mute their phones? She decided she would turn the volume down, that seemed like something commonly done, for instance when someone did not want to disturb others around them. Yes, she decided, she would simply lower the volume so the phone would not be discovered before she wanted it to be. Her plan required it to be found in Justin's room. His foolish decision to leave town had only helped her scheme. She walked quickly to the nightstand and pulled out the drawer.

"What are you doing with Harold's phone?"

The voice surprised Patty. She shut the drawer. Thinking as quickly as she ever had, she turned to Scott Harris standing in the doorway and said, "So you heard it, too?"

Scott was confused. His first thought was that the woman, Patty, had come up to investigate the sound of the ringing telephone. But why did she close the nightstand drawer when he got there? And why had it not rung the dozens of times he'd called over the past twenty-four hours? He'd been in the house most of that time, and each time he'd dialed Harold's phone it had gone into voicemail. *The phone had been off. And now it was on. And Patty Langley had something to do with it.*

"Of course I heard it," Scott answered, remaining in the doorway. He was not about to step aside and let her leave the room. "I've been calling my late husband's phone since yesterday afternoon. I will ask you again, what are you doing with Harold's phone?"

"This is not my room, Mr. Harris."

That threw him off. He hadn't been up to the third floor and would have had no reason to go there. He didn't know which room belonged to which staff member.

"This is Justin's room," Patty explained. "I have reason to believe he left town, and I came in here to see if there was any indication he'd fled."

It was an odd word to use, thought Scott. "Fled? Why would he flee?"

The answer was obvious: Justin Stritch would flee Lambertville because he'd killed Harold and left him in the canal. For money, or drugs, or both.

"I never liked that young man," Patty said. "There was something wrong with him, I could tell the first time I met him. And now he's done something horrible. I'm so sorry, Mr. Harris. I think we should contact the police. Come to my room, we'll call them from there."

Scott was stunned and confused. Everything was happening so quickly he didn't have time to make sense of it. The phone had been off, but now it was on. Justin had kept it but left it behind. Something wasn't right here ...

Patty hurried out and led Scott across the hallway to her room. The sooner she got him away from a crime scene she'd staged, the better. When the police searched Justin's room they would find Harold's phone in one nightstand drawer and his empty cocaine case in another.

She walked to her dresser and retrieved her phone while Scott stepped in, still thinking of everything that had just happened and trying to put it together.

Patty dialed and waited, listening for someone at the police station to pick up.

"It was you," Scott said, staring at her with horror dawning on his face.

Patty heard a voice announce that she had reached the Lambertville Police Station.

"Hello?" said the woman. "Is someone there? May I help you?"

"I'm so sorry," Patty said. "I've dialed a wrong number."

And she hung up the phone.

CHAPTER 55

"What did he say?" asked Kyle as he sped down the street, breaking quickly several times at the speed bumps.

Linda had called the police station and asked for Hoyt. He'd been about to leave, he said, and he only had a moment to hear her out. That changed as Linda quickly told him their suspicions about Patty Langley and her connection to the deaths of Summit and Garland.

"I'm not sure he believed me," Linda replied. "He didn't think I was lying or making it up, don't get me wrong. I could just tell he thought it was ...

"Farfetched?"

"Exactly. And it is, Kyle, when you think about it. Patricia is not an uncommon name, at least it didn't used to be. There could be dozens of Patricia's in Lambertville, even more if you go back in time. Louise Nettles killed herself fifteen years ago. Why get revenge for it now?"

Kyle thought about it a moment, then said, "Maybe that's not really the case. Maybe it only seems like it's all happening now, when in fact it could have been planned for a long time."

"And she was waiting for the opportunity."

"Or she wasn't, and it just presented itself."

"I believe you're right," said Linda. "She couldn't have known Harold Summit was coming to town when she applied for a position with Passion House."

"Or that Garland would stay there. If anything happened by chance, it's his decision to make a reservation. Maybe that's what set it all in motion. She would know who was coming to the house."

"But she wouldn't know what Garland was up to ..."

"Unless he tipped his hand somehow."

"Yes," said Linda, seeing the possibilities. "He may have suspected her involvement all along."

"That would explain his staying at Passion House—he knew she worked there and he wanted to get close to her."

"Too close for his own good," Linda said. "He was closing in on the truth, and she had to kill him, too."

They were approaching the house. Kyle could see Harold Summit's and Scott Harris's car on the street and it reminded him the danger may not be over.

"I think she was the fan Harris told us about."

"The one who kept encouraging them to stay at Passion House."

"That would make sense," said Kyle. "If she'd been stalking Harold Summit for some time and found out he was coming to town for the conference."

"She manipulated them into staying there, then Garland showed up snooping around."

"And it all came crashing together," Linda said. "It's complicated, but murder sometimes is."

"Especially if the murderer is as patient and meticulous as this one seems to be."

Kyle pulled into the driveway, instinctively glancing up at the second floor windows. Was Gladys looking down at them at that moment? Scott Harris? Did Patty see them arrive, and would she have any sense at all that her time was running out … if she was, in fact, the killer? He knew their next encounter could be dangerous—he'd almost ended up dead in the Pride Killer's basement—and he looked up the street hoping to see Hoyt arriving to back them up.

"Where is he?" Kyle asked, watching for the familiar car the sergeant drove. "You don't think he blew us off, do you?"

"Hoyt?" replied Linda. "Not a chance. He'll be here. Just take a deep breath and let's talk to Patty."

Kyle knew she was right. There was no point waiting in the driveway for the cavalry to arrive. There was still a chance they were wrong, that their imaginations had gotten the best of them and Patty was nothing more than a dutiful, humorless housekeeper. But Kyle felt in his bones they were right, and a woman who'd killed three men would not hesitate to kill another.

They heard the gunshot, muffled but distinct. Kyle wasn't sure at first which direction the sound had come from, but Linda knew immediately. She turned her gaze to the third floor windows. A moment later Kyle did the same: someone had fired a weapon upstairs.

"Let's go," Kyle said, and he led them into the house.

CHAPTER 56

"It was you."

Patty had never expected it to come to this. Her plan was unravelling, but she'd come too far to stop now. When Scott Harris realized she had been the one to kill his husband and most likely put an end to Joseph Garland's life, Patty knew she could only move forward with what was left of her scheme. Her options had quickly become very limited, but escape was still possible.

She closed her flip phone after telling the nice woman at the police station that she had misdialed. She pretended to put it back in her dresser drawer, knowing her movements would not cause suspicion in a man who, just moments earlier, would never have imagined her capable of violence on such a scale. She had been nearly invisible for years, working as a helper of one kind or another, human background noise to rich people who could have saved her mother with what it cost them for a long vacation. She kept her voice calm as she opened the top drawer, dropped the phone inside and slipped her hand beneath the clothes she kept there.

"I don't know what you're talking about, Mr. Harris," she said, sliding her fingers around the grip of the Beretta-Wilson 92G she'd purchased when she had first initiated her plan. She had handled guns most of her life and had bought this one on the black market for the express purpose of exacting revenge for her mother's death.

Scott watched her, too shocked by his realization to notice what she was doing.

"You killed Harold," he said. "Probably Gardner, too. Why would you do that? What did Harold ever do to you? Did you need *money*? Was that why you shot him, for a few bills in his wallet?"

Patty pulled her hand from the drawer, pivoted around and pointed the gun at Scott.

Laughing bitterly, she said, "Don't insult me. I wouldn't kill a man for money. I was only taking what he owed me ... his life."

"He *owed* you? He'd never met you!"

Keeping the gun pointed at him, Patty said, "I stand corrected, Mr. Harris. He didn't owe me anything, you're right. But he owed my mother his last breath, just like the one she took before she plunged off the bridge in Stockton. Harold Summit killed my mother."

"That's insane."

"It's not insane, but it is a long story and we don't have time. Otherwise I'd tell you every detail, every desperate plea she made to save her home. I couldn't do it. My brother couldn't do it. But the bank could, and wouldn't. Your husband had the power to help my mother and he refused."

"What about Garland? Did he kill your mother, too?"

"No," said Patty, with a hint of regret in her voice. It was the only indication she gave of remorse. "He made the mistake of being right."

"About what?"

"About me."

Scott stared at her, confused by everything she'd said. He wondered if all of this was more mystery from the man he'd married. Harold had been secretive to say the least, saying little about his life before they met. Was it possible he had been involved in a woman's death? Had there been others? Was Harold Summit even *Harold Summit*?

Scott yanked himself back to the moment. He was standing in front of a dangerous woman, a woman who'd confessed to killing two people. He knew he had to act as he stepped toward Patty.

"You won't shoot me," he said, not sure at all she wouldn't. "You can't get away with this."

Patty pointed the gun at the ceiling and commanded, "Stop!"

The small gun made a large noise in the room as a bullet pierced the ceiling.

Kyle and Linda rushed up the stairs. Kyle was afraid they were too late, that the gunshot they'd heard had put an end to someone's life. But whose?

"Slow down," Linda said, even as she bounded up the steps behind them. "You don't know what you're running into."

Kyle knew she was right. More than once he'd rushed into a situation only to find his life in the balance. If the gun belonged to

Patty — he suspected at this point it did — and she'd shot someone, there was nothing to stop her from shooting Kyle if he barged in. Had the gunshot even come from her room? He was hurrying upstairs on the assumption it had, but maybe it was another room. Justin's? Or Scott's? Or Gladys Finch's?

As they made it to the third floor landing, they heard voices.

"You can't get away with this," Scott said. "I don't even believe you. I think you're a madwoman."

"Oh, I'm mad all right. In fact, I'm furious. I waited a very long time for the opportunity to avenge my mother's death, and anger held that long takes a toll. But I'm feeling much better now, and I'm not afraid to kill you."

"And then what? You won't get far. We're not even alone in this house. The women are just downstairs, probably calling the police right now."

"Let them come," Patty said with sudden resignation. "I don't expect to leave now, it's too late. But I won't need to."

Scott was struck by what she'd said. He was staring at her, wondering if she'd just told him she planned to surrender and be imprisoned for the rest of her life, when Kyle rushed into the doorway. Linda was just behind him.

Patty's arm swung around, bringing the gun to aim at Kyle's chest.

"Don't do this, Patty," Kyle said. "We know what happened, and we understand."

Kyle watched as Patty visibly slumped, her shoulders dropping down, as if a weight had been lifted from her shoulders.

"I don't think you do, Mr. Callahan."

Watching from the hallway behind Kyle, Linda said, "We can try, Patty. Don't let this ruin any more lives."

"The way it ruined my mother's."

"Yes," said Kyle.

Still pointing the gun at him, Patty said, "That's where it all started. A mother I seldom saw, at her request. She was ashamed, no matter how many times I told her not to be. A mother I worried about and tried to look after in my own way, and then the way she was treated — ."

"Terribly," Linda said.

"By the bank," Patty continued, "by Harold Summit and Kevin Lockland. By the town, really. No one helped her, and when she leapt off the bridge ... Did you know her body floated for three days? The reason they knew she jumped in Stockton was because a passing motorist saw her walking across the river but never said anything until there were reports on the news. They described her clothing and he remembered passing a woman dressed like that on the bridge. If it hadn't been for that, they never would have known where she took her life."

Her face darkening, Patty continued, "But she didn't take her life, did she? *They* took it. So I decided to take theirs."

"Joseph Garland had nothing to do with it," Scott said.

Patty glanced at him as if she'd forgotten he was there.

"He should have stayed away," Patty replied. "I could tell he was interested in me, and his foolish curiosity told me why. He was after me, and I struck first, just like I did with Harold Summit. Once I knew you were coming for the writers conference, it wasn't hard to persuade you to stay here. It's as if the stars—or my mother—had set things perfectly in motion."

"Not so perfectly," Scott said. "You've been caught."

Patty's face softened as if in heartbreak or resignation. Then, just as easily, she smiled. "Have I?" she said.

The three of them watched in horror as Patty raised the gun to her head. With no emotion and a face now lacking any expression, she pulled the trigger, sending a bullet racing through her own skull. Blood, bone and brain matter sprayed across the room, peppering Scott Harris as the three of them stared, shocked, at Patty's falling body.

Scott screamed.

Kyle and Linda rushed to the now-dead housekeeper.

Sergeant Bryan Hoyt raced up the stairs.

EPILOGUE

It took weeks for their lives to return to anything resembling a normal state of affairs. Kyle and Danny closed Passion House for a month while they removed any trace of Patty Langley and what she'd done there. Her room had to be professionally cleaned by a service that specialized in crime scenes. Then they had the wood floor refinished and the walls painted. The furniture, too, was replaced. They wanted nothing that had been there when Patty shot herself, nothing that could be said to have been touched by her. They were not trying to erase her, only to remove any lingering evidence of what had happened and what she'd done.

"There will always be an aftertaste," Kyle said one morning, examining the newly painted third floor room. "No matter how many times we try to wash it away."

Danny had agreed, silently taking in the room. He hadn't been there when it happened, but he'd seen Patty's dead body on the floor and heard the commotion when he'd come running over from the guest house. He'd heard the first gunshot, the one that had sent a bullet into the ceiling, but he'd dismissed it as a neighborhood sound. The second gunshot was clearer and he knew it had come from the house. He'd hurried over and heard shouting and crying from upstairs. The first people he'd seen were Gladys and Carol, who'd come out of their room and were standing in the hallway, horrified by what had happened on the floor above them. Gladys was trying to go upstairs while Carol held her back. Danny gently pushed them aside and hurried up the stairs, finding the death scene in Patty's room and Kyle staring helplessly down at her body.

The problem when a murderer kills herself is that it robs the survivors of any sense of justice. Scott Harris and Melissa Lockland would never see Patty Langley held to account in a court of law. Nor would anyone ever know what happened to Kevin Lockland. The one person they all assumed knew his fate was dead. It was the only enduring mystery of the whole affair: Patty had not confessed to harming Kevin, or even having anything to do with his disappearance. It was possible that the two were not connected, that Kevin had in fact embezzled the bank's money and was now enjoying life under an assumed name in some non-extradition country. Or, more likely, his corpse had withered to bones in a grave Patty had dug for him somewhere in the woods.

Scott stayed around a few more days to see the investigation into his husband's death concluded, though he checked out of Passion House and went to a hotel in Flemington. Kyle never saw or heard from him again.

Gladys and Carol left the same night Patty killed herself, although Gladys took Kyle aside and told him she wanted to write a book about the experience. She'd seemed surprisingly energized by the prospect of writing a true crime story in which she was a central character. "Maybe my experience with Harold Summit will pay off after all," she'd told Kyle. "It's the least he could do, don't you think?"

Kyle had not responded. He'd given Gladys a business card and told her to feel free to email him any time. So far she had not.

Justin returned from New York City once he'd seen news reports about the shocking events in sleepy Lambertville. He knew he was in the clear, and the worst he could expect was a scolding from the police about leaving the scene of a crime ... or whatever they called it. He'd been innocent, and innocent people sometimes got out of Dodge.

His employment at Passion House was another story. To his surprise, and to Danny's, Kyle had lobbied to rehire Justin.

"How can you trust him after this?" Danny had asked when Kyle first made his case for bringing Justin back into the house.

"He's a kid," Kyle had said.

"Only someone in his sixties would call a man in his twenties a kid."

"You know what I mean," Kyle had replied. "Emotionally he's a kid, and he may be one for awhile. We can help him grow up."

They knew about Justin's rough childhood, about his rejection by his family and the vagabond life he'd led since leaving home in his teens. Passion House had given him stability, maybe for the first time in his life. Kyle was not ready to throw the young man back to the wolves just yet.

"Fine," Danny had said. "But there will be some new rules

added to the old ones, and if any of them is broken ..."

"He's out."

"Completely and forever."

Justin had been flabbergasted that the couple were willing to take him back, and he'd immediately accepted the offer. He had agreed to their new list of restrictions, the primary one being no involvement of any kind with any houseguest — not a glance, not a touch, not an exchange of phone numbers. Off limits meant off limits.

Kyle had no illusions about the odds for success. Justin was, as Kyle had admitted, a kid in many ways, and kids were going to do as they pleased. But it was worth a try. Justin was as close to a son as they would ever have, and Kyle wanted to give it his best shot.

It didn't take Suzanne Cobb long to contact Kyle after the flurry of media attention died down. She still wanted to add Passion House to her tour of homes in Lambertville, and now she could add a little spice to the description of this particular house.

Finally, after events that had put an indelible stamp on their new life far away from the realities of New York City, a life that was not supposed to include murder and the people who commit it, Kyle and Danny welcomed their first guests back to the house. They made no mention of what had happened, though they quickly discovered most people knew and many of them wanted to stay there for that reason. Maybe they hoped to see the ghost of a housekeeper hovering near the third floor landing, or perhaps they just wanted pictures of themselves spending a few nights in a death house. It was something Kyle and Danny knew they would have to live with, and that was okay. This was their life now, and they loved it.

POSTSCRIPT

Dear David,

So much has happened since I last wrote to you. I thought I'd left that whole murder business behind us in New York, but it wasn't through with me. Maybe I'm just meant to get caught up in these things. Maybe the universe needs me to identify the guilty and bring justice to ... oh, who am I kidding? I'm addicted to solving murders. I hope you'll still be my friend :).

We look forward to seeing you and Elliot in September. Hopefully all this will just be unpleasant memories by then. It's been awful, but also fascinating. Life in Manhattan among eight million other people provided an anonymity you simply can't find in a small town. Everyone may not know everyone else, but they know of you. And now after all this we've become what passes for celebrities in a place like Lambertville. We'll introduce you to the friends we've made, and to Justin the house man, and to our new housekeeper, Lydia. We switched the rooms on the third floor so she wouldn't feel haunted.

We also painted over the mural of the New York City skyline we had in one of the suites. It was time.

I won't keep you longer. I'm thrilled that you're coming. Hopefully there won't be any more bodies turning up before then, but you never know ...

Love,

Kyle

A NOTE FROM MARK

Thank you for taking a ride on the mystery train. I hope you've enjoyed the scenery and the company. If you have a moment to write a review that would be much appreciated. Even a few sentences help other readers discover the books and meet the characters.

Feel free to visit my website at MarkMcNease.com, and join my email list for occasional author updates and complimentary offers. You can find me on Facebook at MarkMcNeaseWriter, on Goodreads, and on Twitter (@markmcnease). I'm always happy to hear directly from readers as well, and I answer every email, so don't be shy, drop me a note anytime (Mark@MarkMcNease.com).

Writing is both my passion and my pleasure, and by the time you read this I'll be working on the next story … and the next.

Yours from the thickening plot,

Mark

Made in USA - North Chelmsford, MA

12.01.2020 1539